When **Kali Anthony** read her first romance novel at fourteen she realised two truths: that there can never be too many happy endings, and that one day she would write them herself. After marrying her own tall, dark and handsome hero, in a perfect friends-to-lovers romance, Kali took the plunge and penned her first story. Writing has been a love affair ever since. If she isn't battling her cat for access to the keyboard, you can find Kali playing dress-up in vintage clothes, gardening, or bushwalking with her husband and three children in the rainforests of South-East Queensland.

Also by Kali Anthony

Revelations of His Runaway Bride
Bound as His Business Deal Bride

Discover more at millsandboon.co.uk.

OFF-LIMITS TO THE CROWN PRINCE

KALI ANTHONY

MILLS & BOON

First published in Great Britain 2021
by Mills & Boon, an imprint of HarperCollins*Publishers* Ltd,
1 London Bridge Street, London, SE1 9GF

www.harpercollins.co.uk

HarperCollins*Publishers*
1st Floor, Watermarque Building,
Ringsend Road, Dublin 4, Ireland

Large Print edition 2021

Off-Limits to the Crown Prince © 2021 Kali Anthony

ISBN: 978-0-263-28906-0

11/21

To my beloved editorcat.

Our last book together.

I miss your paws on my keyboard
every day. Nineteen years
was not enough.

CHAPTER ONE

HANNAH STOOD IN a shaft of bright sunlight at the rear of her studio. A sickening pulse beat in her chest. The dizzying smell of paint and solvent, usually a reminder of everything she loved, threatened to overpower her. She hurried to the window and threw it wide open onto the rambling tangle of a cottage garden. Gulped in the warm, summer's air.

The hollyhocks were in bloom.

Her mother had loved the hollyhocks best of all the flowers growing here.

'Miss Barrington?' A bodyguard. One of three mountains of men who'd arrived minutes before. Two of whom were now stalking through the place, assessing her home for any risk. The one staying with her frowned, no doubt concerned she might be letting in an assailant to harm their employer, whose arrival was imminent. As if she could organise anything like that with the half-hour's warning of his impending visit her agent had given.

'The smell of paint.' She waved her hand about like she was shooing away any offending scents. 'It might irritate His Highness.'

The man nodded, likely satisfied she was thinking of his employer's comfort. They probably wouldn't care about hers, or that in this moment it was like a hand had grabbed round her throat and squeezed. She took another deep breath. The bodyguard stationed himself at the doorway separating her studio from the rest of the house and crossed his arms as though he were guarding *her*. Did she look as if she were about to run?

Tempting, but there was nowhere else to go.

Her country cottage, the family home. Her safe place and haven was all she had left of her parents. She looked around the bright room she'd made her studio when she'd been old enough to move out on her own. People said she was crazy to come back here, away from the city, to a place tired from nine years of tenants. But people didn't understand. Even though there'd been a fresh lick of paint, no one had covered over the marks on the wall in the laundry where her parents had notched her height over the years. The low-ceilinged kitchen remained unrenovated, a place where they'd sat to eat their meals and laughed. The whole place sang with those memories. The happy and the devastating.

The burn of tears pricked her eyes. Now all this was at risk. Her aunt and uncle had been her guardians. Looked after her inheritance when her parents had died. Taken in the broken teenager she'd become. Sure, they'd been distant rather than cruel, never having wanted children of their own and not knowing how to deal with her. But she'd trusted them, and her uncle's betrayal still cut deep and jagged. An investment she hadn't wanted gone terribly wrong. Almost everything, lost. Her father would be trying to claw his way out of the grave over the way his brother had behaved towards his only niece.

Everything seemed tenuous in this moment. Nothing else had broken her. Not her parents' death in the accident, not the loss of her horse and everything she loved. She'd clambered out of the well of grief on her own. Sure, her fingertips might have been bloody, nails torn, the scars carved into the soul of her waiting to open at any given moment. But to have to sell this, the little farm where she'd lived some of the best days of her life? That would crack her open and no king's horses or men would ever be able to put those pieces back together again.

Perspiration pricked at the back of her head, a droplet sliding beyond the neck of her shirt, itching her skin. She moved closer to the window. Fished a hair tie from her jeans pocket, scraped her hair back and tied it up in a rough topknot.

The bodyguard looked down at her. Crossed his arms. 'You seem nervous.'

How could she tell him that his employer's past and her own were inextricably bound? That his employer was the last person she wanted to see, because he was a reminder of the worst day of her life? Of teenage dreams destroyed?

'I've never met a prince before.' It wasn't *exactly* a lie. 'And I haven't had time to tidy up.'

The bodyguard's gaze roved over her in a disapproving kind of way. She looked down at her hands. Nails short and blunt. Cuticles ingrained with paint. She grabbed an old rag and wet it with solvent, rubbing at her fingers in a vain effort to clean them. Perfect princes probably wouldn't admire commoners with filthy hands. Not that she was seeking admiration, but still.

She supposed she had to keep up some kind of an appearance. After a short effort she dropped the now dirty rag on the tabletop and sniffed at her fingers, which smelled like pine.

She held them up. 'Better?'

The bodyguard grunted.

Hannah checked her phone. Still some time. She picked out a slender paintbrush and stood back from her easel. Her art usually calmed her, a way to lose herself in colour and light. Nothing could touch her when she was in the flow of a portrait. She tried to loosen the death grip of her fingers. Dipped her brush into some paint. A swipe of Tasman blue, a touch of titanium white. She frowned. The eyes in this portrait gave her trouble. Too much sadness, not enough twinkle. She reached out her brush to add a dash of colour near the pupil, trying to ignore the tremor in her hand.

The cheery tinkle of a doorbell rang through the room. Hannah's paintbrush slipped from her fingers and clattered to the floor, leaving smudges of blue paint on the old boards.

The burn of bile rose to her throat. He was early. She left the portrait and wiped her damp palms on her jeans.

'Remember to curtsey,' the bodyguard said.

The teeth of anger bit her then, at this man's disdain when she was the one being imposed upon today. She'd said no to this commission when it had first been proposed months ago, before she had had any idea how bad her finances were. His employer had ignored her refusal. It was just like saying no to her uncle when presented with a speculative investment. He'd ignored her too. She gritted her teeth, hating that these people hadn't listened to her, as if her opinion were meaningless. But even though things were bad it didn't mean she had to grin and bear it.

Hannah stalked up to the man guarding the doorway and glared. He towered over her but she didn't care. She wasn't going to be pushed around, by anyone. Looming bodyguard *or* prince.

'I do have a concept of manners. And I understand how to behave around royalty.'

The man didn't move, but his eyes widened a fraction as if in surprise. Good.

A murmur of voices drifted down the hall. The tap of fine leather on floorboards grew louder. She backed further into the room, tried to swallow the knot rising in her throat but her mouth was dry.

A shadow appeared in the hall behind more security. Grew and grew till it took human shape, striding through the doorway.

'His Royal Highness, Crown Prince of Lasserno,' the bodyguard announced.

Alessio Arcuri.

More beautiful than she'd remembered, though the recollection was coloured by her youth at the time. Then, she'd only caught thrilling glimpses of the handsome, fairy-tale prince, a rider on the showjumping circuit. The young man her teenage heart had crushed over with a terrifying ferocity. Now, she could fully appreciate the height and breadth of him. His severe yet tantalising and lush mouth. The perfection of his aquiline nose. The caramel of his sun-bronzed skin. The shock of his thick, dark hair. She could pretend her admiration was one of an artist surveying his commanding masculine shape. But who was she kidding? This was a distinctly female attraction to a male in his absolute prime.

After nine years, she still felt like that giddy teenager.

It made her prickly all over. Too big for her

skin. She wanted to shed parts of herself like a husk, and come out more sparkling, more polished. Just *more*. Because she didn't need a mirror to realise she looked like some ruffian and he looked as if he'd walked straight from a red carpet.

She resented his perfection, when his snap visit with little warning meant she'd had no time to tidy her own appearance. His exquisitely cut suit in the deepest of navy, a pristine white shirt. Red and blue tie in the finest of glowing silk. She was sure she stared before remembering her manners, dipping into a curtsey. 'Your Highness.'

'Signorina Barrington.' He canted his head in a way that suggested she was *adequate*, then motioned to the man standing behind him. 'This is my private secretary, Stefano Moretti. He's been communicating with your agent.'

The other man was almost as perfectly attired and presented as his employer. Attractive, but without the indefinable presence of the Prince. She nodded to him. He smiled back.

'Welcome to my home and studio. It's a surprise and I'm underprepared. I didn't expect royalty to drop by today. Would you like a tea?' She motioned to a battered table in the corner of her studio, the ancient electric kettle, some chipped cups.

Alessio looked to where she'd indicated, gaze sliding over the table as though viewing a sad still life. No one came here—this was her private space—so there was no one to bother about damaged crockery. Personal sittings took place in her public studio on the outskirts of London. The one she'd only recently given up, her uncle's actions meaning it was an extravagance she couldn't afford. Yet seeing the room with Alessio in it reminded her how tattered and worn it seemed. She'd never worried before. This was her home. But all it took was a perfectly pressed prince to bring into screamingly sharp relief how threadbare her life had become.

'Tea? No. I was in the area purchasing some horses, and, since you've been ignoring my secretary's requests...' His voice had the musical lilt of Italian spoken in a glorious baritone. Honeyed tones she could listen to for hours. The voice of a leader that would echo on castle walls. One whose dictates would invariably be followed by most.

Not by her. She wasn't this prince's subject.

'I haven't been ignoring them. My answer was clear.'

He hesitated for a second, cocked his head as if he were thinking. She had the curious sensation of being a specimen under glass.

'Have we met before?'

The high slash of his cheekbones, the strong brows. The sharply etched curve of his tempting lips. Eyes of burnt umber framed by the elegant curl of lamp black lashes. Hannah had never formally met him, but she'd never forgotten him from the showjumping circuit. Alessio Arcuri was the kind of man to leave you breathless. The fearlessness as he rode. The sheer arrogance that he would make every jump successfully. And he did. Horse and rider the embodiment of perfection.

It was why she and her friend had been chattering away in the back of the car on that terrible day. Gossiping about why he'd retired from competition at the age of twenty-two, much to their teenage devastation. Now, it seemed so young. Back then, he'd been the epitome of an adult and everything a clueless sixteen-year-old craved to be. How he appeared to know, in a way that was absolute, his place in the world. The utter confidence of him, when Hannah was still trying to find her bearings. Then she dropped out of riding too, the deaths of her parents and her horse too much to bear. And she'd tried not to think about Prince Alessio Arcuri since.

At least, until her agent's call a little over half an hour ago, when all the memories she'd bottled up had come flooding back.

'No. We haven't met.' Not exactly. He'd been handing out the first prize at a showjumping event she'd competed in after his retirement had been announced. Her friend had won that day, Hannah a close second. Unusual for her but Beau had been off, as if her horse were foreshadowing the devastating events of only hours later. She'd been so envious of that first-prize ribbon. How she'd coveted the handshake Alessio had given to her friend. Craved for him to acknowledge her. Then their eyes had met. Held. And for one perfect, blinding second her world had stopped turning.

After what had come later in the afternoon, those desires seemed childish. It had taken another terrible moment on that day for the world to stop turning a second time. It hadn't restarted.

His being here brought back too many memories of a split second when all her innocence and faith in the good of the world had ended. Riding passenger in the car driven by her friend's parents. Rounding a corner, littered debris...the... carnage. Car and horsebox destroyed. Everything she'd loved, gone. A freak accident. A tractor in the wrong place on a narrow country road. Hannah flinched. Shut her eyes tight against the horrible vision running like a stuttering film reel in her head.

'Are you all right, Signorina Barrington?'

She opened her eyes again. Nodded. Breathed. Stitched up the pain in her heart where it would stay for ever. Hannah didn't want to go back to that time, and if Alessio truly remembered he might start asking questions. She couldn't deal with them, not now.

Alessio looked at his bodyguards, standing as a brooding presence in the corner. Said something in rapid Italian and they bowed and left the room. The atmosphere relaxed a fraction.

'I'm here to discuss you painting my portrait.'

Hannah clasped her hands behind her back. 'As my agent would have told you, I have a number of commissions...'

Alessio stepped towards her and she was

forced to look up because, whilst she wasn't tiny, he dwarfed her. He was even more astonishing up close. Nothing marred his features. It was as if no part of the man would deign to be anything less than polished and perfect. He held her transfixed with those velvety brown eyes of his. Till looking at him any more left her head spinning.

He must have taken her silence as reticence.

'Your fee. I'll double it. And I'm a prince, so...'

She stepped back. It was either that or lean into him and all his solidity in a moment when she felt a little broken. 'I know what you are.'

What was she doing? Crucifying herself, that was what. She needed this commission, but she couldn't help herself. She'd made a promise when she first started painting, that she'd only take the jobs she wanted. Trying to establish a connection with your subject could prove taxing some days. In the early stages after her parents died she'd drawn them incessantly, terrified that the memory of how they looked would fade. Day and night she sketched, to perfect them so she could never forget. It had exhausted her, the obsession. Made her ill. Sometimes it still did when she became engrossed with a commission. It was why she chose so carefully.

Alessio Arcuri would never be a careful choice. Any connection with him could break her.

'Then I promise if you paint my portrait I'll ensure everyone knows who *you* are. So far those you've painted have been…inconsequential.'

Portraiture had never been about accolades, but about preserving memories. The minutiae, the nuance of a person. Sure, she was paid well for what she did, but it was *never* about simply being paid. It was about ensuring people weren't forgotten.

She looked at the portrait of the older woman currently on her easel. A believer in justice, lover of barley sugar and Yorkshire tea. 'I wouldn't say a judge is *nobody.* The law's important, as is doing the right thing. But I mostly like painting pictures of people the world overlooks. They deserve their moment to be seen, to be remembered. You're seen all the time.'

Alessio shrugged. That movement seemed out of place on a man who appeared only to move when absolutely necessary. 'Is anyone truly seen? The press often tries to paint pictures of me and they're rarely right.'

'What picture do they try to paint?' The cool command? The lack of emotion? She could imagine they'd claim he was more automaton than real and relish finding the tiniest chink in his gleaming armour to take him down.

Alessio raised an eyebrow. 'You haven't looked me up on the internet? I thought you were re-nowned for knowing your subjects.'

'You're not my subject so I haven't needed to know you.'

'The judge.' He inspected the painting, eyes narrowing as he stared at the woman on the can-vas. 'That portrait tells stories. I want you to tell mine. You're the best. No one could see me like you could.'

Part of her wanted to mine the essence of him, because people fascinated her. But doing so had a cost and she wasn't sure she was prepared to pay it when Alessio reminded her of everything she'd lost.

'"The best" is subjective. I have terms for every-one I paint. My agent tells me you refused mine.'

Sue had been clear. You didn't say *no* to a prince. Hannah had to keep her options open… She knew what those ominous words meant. Once her uncle's duplicity had been discovered,

this meeting with the Prince had become necessary. Resented, but necessary none the less.

'I'm here now,' Alessio said. The hard, uncompromising set of his jaw told her he might regis-
ter what she said but he wasn't really listening.

She turned her back on him and walked to a
paint-splattered desk on which her palette and
scattered half-used tubes of oil paint were strewn
in the haphazard way of this whole room. She
opened a drawer and pulled out a few papers,
then walked back to where he stood and thrust
them in his direction. He took them from her
paint-ingrained fingers. Flicked through.

'Am I a cat or dog person?' His eyebrows rose
in disbelief. 'What is this?'

She took time with her subjects. The questionnaire was one small part. There were personal
sittings, the live sketching. She'd been comfortable with each person she'd painted so far. Had
liked them and their quirks in their own way.
But Alessio Arcuri? She wasn't sure she could.
A person's eccentricities, no matter how small,
gave them personality. How could she do justice to this man, who didn't seem to have a quirk
about him? He dazzled like a flawless gemstone.

'Those questions are the reason I'm so good at what I do. I get to know my subjects. Intimately.'

At the last word his eyes widened a fraction. Surely he wouldn't think… Heat rushed to her cheeks. The corner of his mouth kicked up a minute fraction. The moment counted in milliseconds and then it was gone, before his attention returned to the paper in his hands. But even those seconds had her heart racing in an attempted getaway.

"What is your best childhood memory?" "Your worst?"' A frown marred his forehead. He thrust the pages back at her. 'No. If the press got hold of this—'

'They won't.' She ignored his outstretched arm. 'I read it, then destroy it. I also sign non-disclosure agreements for those who want them. No information has *ever* reached any press outlet from me. You could take some time and fill out my questions right here.'

He seemed to stand even taller now, imposing like the prince he was. She could even imagine the gleaming crown on his head.

'All these people you paint. The press has no interest in them. Me? I'm royalty. You know how tabloids clamour for stories. I give them none. But this?' He waved his hands over the offending document as if he were trying to bat away some pestilential bug set on biting him. 'I don't answer twenty questions, for anyone.'

'There are eighteen questions. But the number isn't important. You can *tell* me the answers.'

He dropped the papers on the table next to him. 'You're a stranger.'

And that was the way it would stay for ever, even though there was something about this tussle Hannah began to enjoy. A tiny thrill that his interest still held, no matter how she pushed. It told her he *really* wanted her to paint him, stroking an ego she didn't realise needed attention. What would her sixteen-year-old self think now?

That young girl would think all her dreams had come true.

'Here's the thing. Doing this allows me to paint at my best. The type of picture you seem to desire, seeing as you're still standing in my studio. You want me to paint your portrait, then…double my fee and answer my questions.' She rose up, stiffening her spine to match him. If he was playing the prince card then she'd pull a queen on him, because this studio was *her* domain and she ruled here exclusively. 'You can take it or leave it.'

Alessio hadn't expected a warm welcome, but he'd expected something more polite than this. Certainly, she'd curtseyed as expected. A seemingly respectful bow of the head when he was sure none was meant, because her eyes had flashed a kind of warning, the whole of her bristling like some disapproving hedgehog. Cute, but all spike and prickle. Right now, she stood framed by the light from the windows behind her. Dark hair mussed in an unruly topknot. Dressed in a blue and white striped men's shirt with a frayed collar, cuffs pushed back on her forearms, smeared and smudged with paint. Loose, ripped jeans. Trainers as paint-spattered as the rest of her.

Dishevelled and all the more enticing for it.

'I tend not to accede to ultimatums,' he said. Though he admired hers more than he'd admit. She'd hold her own with some of the best of his courtiers, this woman.

She glared at him, no respect meant there at all, and their eyes truly met. Hers were green, perhaps. Arresting. Their depth and swirls of colour transfixed him. She carried the world in that luminous gaze and something drove him to discover what lay behind it, when discovering anything about her other than whether she was prepared to paint his portrait was impossible. He pushed the interest aside.

Ruthlessly.

'I tend not to *give* ultimatums.' Her voice was deeper than he'd expected. Almost…aristocratic in its tone. It feathered his spine the way a stroke of her paint-ingrained fingers might. And in these moments he couldn't avoid the pressing sense of déjà vu, as if he was missing something. Everything about her seemed…strangely familiar.

She claimed not to know him but was as skittish as a colt in spring when he'd first mentioned it. Perhaps it had something to do with his security detail. They tended to suck the air out of the place with their professional brand of malevolence, which was why he'd asked them to leave. Stefano stayed, of course. Alessio didn't spend time alone with women he didn't know, not any more. There would be no ugly rumours. Everyone who surrounded him was carefully vetted and explicitly trusted. He'd learned lessons about putting faith in the wrong person. His father might have courted the press with his outrageous behaviour but Alessio gave them nothing.

'We seem to be at a stalemate,' he said.

She cocked her head. Raised her eyebrows. 'Yet you're *still* here.'

Perhaps there was an answer which could accommodate everybody. His life had been spent trying to find solutions to every problem, mostly regarding his father. He'd become an expert at it, spending his hours working to silence hints at his father's worst excesses, the rumours about the missing gems from the crown jewels. As for Hannah Barrington—when he'd asked Stefano to find the best portrait artist in the world he hadn't expected it to be a reclusive young woman of twenty-five, whose paintings looked as if they contained the experience and insight of a life long-lived. On viewing her portfolio of work, he knew he'd found the person for his portrait.

He turned to his secretary. As he did so, Hannah seemed to start towards him, then checked herself. Interesting. Did she think he was about to leave? Perhaps she wanted this commission more than she was prepared to admit? If so, everyone had their price. And he was prepared to pay a high price for her. Hannah Barrington was the best, and he'd have nothing less. *'Start as you mean to finish,'* his English nanny had used to say, teaching him her language as a young boy and what it meant to be leader of his principality. Better a foreigner who knew the value of royalty and duty, than his father, who valued none of those things. The lessons Alessio had learned at his knee were all about excess, indulgence and infidelity. Not the qualities of the leader Alessio wished to aspire to be.

Stefano raised an eyebrow as Alessio approached looking far too entertained at developments. His friend, partner in crime in the years gone by and now private secretary remained his most trusted confidant.

'It gives me great satisfaction that there's one woman in the world who's immune to your charms,' Stefano said in their native Italian, presumably so Signorina Barrington couldn't understand. 'Although you're not being charming today.'

Whilst he knew it was rude, Alessio didn't switch to English, and wouldn't until he had his solution. 'I need to know the state of my diary. I've *no* need to charm anyone.'

He'd set aside that reputation years ago. Alessio would admit in his youth he had relished in the position his birth gave him. He wasn't proud of those things now, especially the string of women who had cemented his playboy reputation. *Like father, like son*, the press used to say. A creep of disgust curled inside him. Not now. An advantageous marriage to a perfect princess was next on his agenda. To give Lasserno the stability it had lacked since his mother's death. Some heirs to continue his line. The royalty in Lasserno would soon be feted in its perfection, not mocked for its all too human failings. That was his mission, and he would succeed.

Stefano pulled up Alessio's diary, showed it to him. Busy, but not impossible.

'Your problem is that you don't like people saying "no" to you,' Stefano murmured. In English this time.

How many times had he tried to stop his father? Curb his behaviour? It was what he'd ostensibly been brought home to do, ripped out of his life showjumping and studying in the UK when his mother had fallen ill, because at least when she was well she'd formed some sort of brake on his father's worst excesses. And yet when he'd brought up ideas to reinvigorate the economy and tourism in a country whose beauty and natural riches were equal to anywhere in their close neighbour, Italy, he'd been met with disparaging refusal. No answers as to why his ideas wouldn't work. Nothing at all.

Stefano was correct. Alessio didn't like being told *no* on things he was right about. Not without a sensible reason. Since his father's abdication he'd not heard that cursed word from one of his government or advisors. It was…gratifying in a way he could never have imagined. A vindication of all he'd been trying to achieve over the years.

Alessio turned his attention to Hannah. Checked his watch. 'I will not write answers to your questionnaire, but I do have some limited time in my schedule.'

Time he could control. Leaking of information he couldn't.

A slight frown creased her brow and he wasn't sure whether the disapproval was back, or whether something else was at play.

'Then I can't—'

'My calendar is free of more onerous engagements. You wish to know me to paint my portrait? You'll travel to Lasserno. Become my official artist for two weeks. Follow me and learn about me. It should be enough.'

He could almost *sense* the weight of Stefano's incredulous stare but he didn't much care what his best friend thought at this moment. The woman in front of him had his complete focus. The plump, perfect peach colour of her mouth. The rockpool-green of her eyes. Eyes which stared deep inside as if they saw the heart of him. Eyes a man could drown in and die happy if he allowed himself, which Alessio could never do. It was no matter. He was used to compartmentalising that side of himself. There would be *no* rumours of improper behaviour on his part. His life was one of supreme control, Lasserno his only mistress.

She planted her paint-stained hands on her hips. 'Now, look. That's—'

'Not your process. I'm aware. This will be better.'

He could get anyone else to paint him. Most people would climb over themselves to take the commission and the accolades it would afford.

In coming to his decision he'd been shown the work of many artists who were all superb and could acquit themselves admirably. The minute he saw Hannah Barrington's work, he knew. It was her he must have. No one else would do. And yet here she stood, utterly uncompromising. As if she were still intent on *refusing* him. The challenge of it set his pulse beating hard. He'd not felt anything like it since the last time he'd taken his stallion, Apollo, over the high fence behind the vineyards on the castle grounds.

'I have other clients.' Whilst her hands were still firmly on her hips, her teeth worried furiously at her bottom lip.

'You have an agent. She can tell clients you're painting a portrait of a prince. They'll understand, because my patronage will increase the value of their own pictures. I promise, this commission will be the *making* of you.'

'It's *two weeks* away from my home. You're not the only busy person in the room.' All the glorious fire in her, such a contrast to the cool mint of her eyes. For a moment he wished he were an ordinary man who could explore these ordinary desires, but that was a folly he would not indulge in.

This portrait, the *perfect* portrait, would show the world exactly how he meant to carry on his role as a leader. It would be the best. *He* would be the best prince Lasserno had seen in its long and proud history. He would write over his father's legacy, scratching it out in a neat and perfect script till it disappeared and was forgotten.

Hannah was the first piece in a larger puzzle. Time to sweeten the deal. To make it irresistible.

'I'll offer you *five* times your normal fee for the inconvenience.'

Her nostrils flared, and her eyes sparked at the mention of increasing her fee. Avarice was something he understood, a common currency, and he was happy to fuel it so long as it was legal and he got his way in the end. His former girlfriend, Allegra, was a perfect study in how money won over loyalty. Luckily he had more than the reporter had offered for a story on how his father had been picking gems from the crown jewels and giving them away as favours. Replacing them with paste. He'd never forgotten the lessons learned in that episode about unburdening yourself to the wrong person.

Hannah opened her mouth to speak. Alessio held up his hand, because there was more.

'*But* you accompany me as official palace artist in residence. You won't receive a better offer from any other client,' he said with a smile which felt like victory. 'Take it…or leave it.'

CHAPTER TWO

HANNAH SQUIRMED, TRYING to get comfortable in the chair on which she'd been directed to sit by Alessio's secretary. Who'd have thought something so ornate, with all its carved wood and brocade upholstery, could be so hard and uncompromising? A bit like its owner, and maybe that was the point. Being left like this to await *His Highness* held all the appeal of that one time she'd been sent to the headmaster at her austere boarding school for *'having your head in the clouds rather than in reality, Miss Barrington'.* No sympathy for the plight of a teenager who'd been ripped from everything she knew and loved.

She'd received a detention that day for telling him that reality sucked. After losing her parents, her imagination was a safer place to reside. Drawing obsessively. Trying to remember every line of their faces as the memories faded. The love she saw when they'd looked at her, rather than the feigned interest of her uncle and aunt.

She shut those thoughts down. They had no place here.

Hannah stared at the looming oak doors of what she'd been told was the Prince's office. Everything seemed to loom in an ominous way here, in this imposing castle which rose from a landscape of olive groves and vineyards in turreted glory. Hannah worried at a tiny thread which dared to loosen itself from the chair's rich brocade. Her imagination didn't seem safe now, with Hannah spending far too much time dreading the shape of the next fortnight. Alessio was a reminder of that day, of all she'd lost. She took a deep breath, chased away old memories of her time before the accident when her reality had allowed her to dream of princes who set her heart fluttering complicated rhythms. Of a time when her parents had said she could have anything she wanted if she dared to dream, such as one day riding for her country as Alessio did. Thoughts of a time *before* had started nipping her heels with her arrival in Lasserno polished, primped and plucked. Sue had taken to Prince Arcuri's invitation with an unhealthy enthusiasm, seeing it as her only chance to turn Hannah into something she was not—a woman of the world.

Hannah looked down at her hands. They were almost as unrecognisable as the rest of her with manicured nails, moisturised cuticles and not a stain of paint to be seen. Her hair had been stylishly trimmed, and brows sculpted to perfection. At home in England Hannah never needed much. No fancy dresses or make-up. Simple food on the table. She didn't go out. Her life was paint and canvas, palette and brush. Her art was her work and her work was her life, but Alessio's commission dictated there were some things she required.

New clothes to suit the list of occasions he'd sent were packed in a large suitcase. Well, not exactly new. Her uncle's duplicity meant haunting charity shops, but with a bit of inventive tailoring she'd come up with a wardrobe that would satisfy the eyewatering requirements of His Royal Highness, the proverbial pain in her backside. But, standing in front of a mirror this morning in her jeans and boots, tailored navy jacket with crisp white blouse, she'd been unrecognisable. Hannah didn't know who the person was, staring back at her. She wasn't sure she liked it.

One of the oak doors glided open. Her stomach twisted into sharp, complicated knots as Stefano stepped into the hall. She'd come to know him a little over the past week when she'd been getting everything in order to come here. His missives had been polite, his manner on the phone efficient, sympathetic and kind, but she'd been able to glean nothing about his employer from him. All she'd discovered had been found online.

That the press believed the man's austere demeanour hid greater sins.

'His Highness will see you now.'

She walked through the open door and it thudded shut behind her. She took a few steps over the plush crimson carpet then stopped, overwhelmed by the sheer scale of the room.

Magnificent frescoes covered the ceiling. Adorning the walls were paintings of what must have been former rulers. Uniformed and striking a pose, warriors on horseback with swords drawn, all staring down in their own princely kind of way from their vast gilded frames. But more magnificent than anything else in the opulent space was a man lit up in a shaft of sunlight like a god. Standing behind an expansive antique desk, he outshone any of his forebears, more regal than all of them put together in his dark suit and ultramarine tie.

She almost forgot herself as she stared, Alessio's black hair gleaming, his intense eyes hooded and assessing, the slash of one aristocratic eyebrow raised quizzically. What were all those rules she had to remember again? Sensible thought had fled. Before she made a total fool of herself, she gave a hasty curtsey because it seemed the thing to do, then hurried towards the desk. He made some dismissive waving kind of motion which she took to mean, *Have a seat*, and sank into the armchair opposite. Just in time, because her legs seemed like overcooked noodles in their inability to hold her up. The corner of his mouth threatened an almost smile, and her heart skipped a few beats, its rhythm constantly out of synch in his presence.

'You had a good flight?'

'The royal jet was an extravagance.' With all its buttery leather and plush carpets. She'd been treated like a princess by the efficient flight crew. 'I could have flown commercial.'

'Think of it as a reward for uprooting your life over the next fortnight. I trust your other clients weren't too disappointed about your upcoming absence.'

She noticed it wasn't spoken as a question.

Positively enthusiastic had been the general response. The Prince had been irritatingly right. They all saw the value of their own portraits increasing because she'd agreed to take on the commission. She'd been surprised they hadn't met her at the airport and thrown streamers in a grand farewell as she boarded the aircraft. She shook her head, which earned her another tilt of his mouth in what she suspected was Alessio's version of a smile. Her silly little heart tripped over itself at how the tiny move softened every harsh feature on his face to something more. More handsome, more vital, more...human.

But this man wasn't human, he was a prince. Unattainable. Untouchable. As a young girl she dreamed of princes, but dreams didn't make reality. She could never forget it.

He sat in the leather chair at his desk. Even that move was perfectly executed. 'I thought we would have a brief discussion about expectations whilst you're here.'

'You mean, in addition to the indexed folder I was given on the plane?' There seemed to be so many dizzying rules and requirements, how to address staff, what to wear. An agenda for almost every minute of the day. It was no wonder the man in front of her looked so serious. There didn't seem to be a moment when he sat still, apart from when he was asleep, because the time he 'retired' had been scheduled in as well. When was there ever space to simply *be*? Sit on a comfortable couch, with a warm drink in hand, and stare out of a window at a view. Imagine… a different life.

She looked at him, sitting straight and perfect and still. Not a hair out of place. Not a wrinkle in his shirt. As if he were carved out of painted stone. It seemed he was more statue than flesh and blood.

How exhausting.

'At all times, your behaviour reflects on me. I ask you to recognise that and adjust your manner accordingly.'

She sat up a little straighter in her seat, the heat flaming in her cheeks. A slice of something hot and potent cutting through her. 'I might not be aristocracy but I wasn't brought up in a shoebox. I know how to behave in civilised society.'

He cocked his head. Those umber eyes of his

fixed on her with an almost otherworldly intensity. 'How gratifying to hear. When we're in public together, you'll walk behind me. The only woman who will ever walk at my side is my princess.'

'So where is this princess now? Do I get to meet her too?'

'There is no princess yet.'

'Shame. I thought she might be able to give me some tips. Juicy gossip even.'

The perfect Prince's eyes narrowed. His lips tightened.

'There is no *juicy gossip*. My life is my country. My country is my life. That is all you need to know.' His voice was ice. The cold blast of a winter gale. A tremor shuddered through her at the chill of his tone. She almost believed there was nothing more to him than this and didn't know why that thought left an ache deep inside, because it struck her as sad.

'Duly noted,' she said. Her answer seemed to mollify him. He gave a curt nod in reply.

'When we are in public you will refer to me as Your Highness or Sir.'

'I've read the rulebook, though there was one thing it didn't address.' She leaned back into the soft upholstery of the armchair and tried to relax, though nothing about the man sitting opposite encouraged her to do so. 'What about when we're in private?'

'There will be no *"in private".*'

Hannah looked about the vast room, through the windows that gave a view of rolling hills and olive groves beyond. Pencil pines spearing upwards from a garden like dark green sentinels. 'We're alone now.'

'Stefano.'

'Sì?'

Hannah whipped round. Stefano stood just inside the closed doors of the room. He gave her a wry smile. She turned back to Alessio. Crossed her legs. Clasped her hands over her knee. He followed her every move, almost as if he were cataloguing her.

'Where were you hiding the poor man—in a cupboard?'

'There is a chair, in an alcove, inside the door. However, where Stefano sits is immaterial. What is material is that we will not be alone.'

'Then how am I meant to begin the process of painting your portrait?'

'I would have thought it quite easy. Brush, canvas.'

She shook her head. 'I can't work with strangers…loitering about. Portrait painting is a contract between two people. The artist and the subject. Of its nature it's…intimate. I—'

'So you have said before. You don't get to dictate terms, Signorina Barrington.'

No. There was a way she worked and, although she tried to be a little flexible, the way he spoke to her rankled. She clenched her hands a bit harder round her knees.

'It's a wonder you don't pick up a brush and paint yourself… *Your Highness.*'

Everything about him seemed impassive, inscrutable. Having barely any expression, his face was marked only by a cool, regal kind of presence. She could get the measure of most people, but never the measure of him. Even as a far younger man, there'd been nothing on his face to tell what he might be thinking. Like a blank canvas waiting for the first, defining brushstroke.

'If I could, I would.' Alessio sat back in his leather chair, which creaked as his weight shifted. Steepled his fingers. 'However, there's a reason

I engaged you and that's because you're reputedly the best. I will have *nothing* but the best.'

A vice of tightness crushed her chest. Right now, she wasn't at her best. What her uncle had done had floored her. She had thought she could at least trust her family. Now she was being forced to take this commission due to circumstance, which was not the way she'd ever worked. What would her parents have thought of all this? They believed they'd ensured the security and comfort of their only daughter and she'd let it slip away by being too absorbed in her art and not keeping a close enough eye on things, till it was too late and the money gone. The threat of tears burned the back of her nose. Even after nine years the grief still hovered close. All these things had weighed on her and right now her thoughts were not about colour and light, or the gentle tilt of someone's almost smile, but on survival again.

Though that might suit a painting of this man. The expressionless quality. She could try losing herself in that, a simplicity which meant she didn't need to fight the canvas to find the heart of him. Because there was nothing in his face she could grasp, apart from the impact of his sheer masculine beauty. Like the statue of David. Exquisite, perfect, coldly etched. She doubted he had a warm, beating heart. But in the end to do her best, to paint what critics said she was renowned for, she needed *something* curious for her brushstroke to shape. Some expression to show the person before her was man, not marble. Because sadly she was a portrait artist, not a sculptor.

She stood and walked towards a wall on which one portrait hung, of a man sitting on a golden chair. Old. Imposing.

'I didn't invite you to leave your seat.' Alessio's voice was cool as the blast of air-conditioning on a hot summer's day. She wheeled round. He was still seated himself. Was there something in that dossier she'd been given to read about this? She couldn't remember, though the man probably wasn't used to having anyone turn their back on him. Still, whilst he was a prince, she was a grown woman. She'd accord him the respect required because of the quirk of his birth, but asking for permission to stand?

Ridiculous.

'That's going to make things difficult if I need to ask you for permission whenever I have to do something. Your Highness, may I drink my glass of water? Your Highness, may I use the bathroom? Your Highness, may I apply this charcoal to paper?'

He swivelled his chair to face her, gazing at her with an intriguing intensity, as if she were an olive he was about to skewer in the tines of a martini fork.

'There are rules by which the palace and my country is run. Those rules keep chaos away from the door. In this place, you follow mine.'

'That's not going to work when I'm trying to draw or paint you.'

'We'll see.'

'So let me ask.' She swept her hand across the room, taking in all the ancestors hanging on his walls, staring out at them disapprovingly. 'Given you have an opinion on all things, what do you want your portrait to look like?'

He frowned, making the merest of creases in his perfectly smooth forehead, but she saw it none the less. 'Isn't it your job to decide?'

'How about that one?' She pointed to a man on horseback in a grand uniform braided with gold. There was no emotion on his face at all, nor in the way he watched the room impassively, with dark eyes. All the emotion was contained in the wild eyes of the rearing bay on which he sat, as if it were nothing but a plump little pony and he was going for a quiet afternoon ride. 'He looks suitably warrior-like.'

She could imagine Alessio that way. She'd seen him ride, the fearlessness which made everyone hold their breath. The memory was like a stab at her heart, a constant reminder of everything she'd lost. Because she'd loved flying over jumps too. Encouraging herself and her horse to go hard, be better.

'Since we're not at war, no.'

Relief crashed over her like waves in a storm. Not on horseback, then.

'What about him?' She pointed to another grand portrait. The man on the gilded seat. With distant eyes and a hard mouth. His demeanour stern, looking like a disapproving relative. One hand clasping a gleaming sceptre. The other gripping the arm of the chair on which he sat. A large, bejewelled ring adorning his finger. Not a relaxed pose, even though you couldn't tell from his face. The face told her nothing. 'He's sitting on a throne. Very regal and proper.'

'The throne is…no.'

Alessio stood and walked towards her. His flawless grey suit gripping the masculine angles of his body. Every movement long and fluid. It was clear this was his domain and he was comfortable in it. He moved next to her. Not too close, but any distance was not far enough. He had a presence. Not threatening, but overwhelming, as if everything gravitated towards him. She swallowed, her mouth dry, her heart tripping over itself.

'Then who do you want to be? How do you want to be seen?'

He stared down at her. Like a ruler lording over his subject. Except she'd *never* be that. But still, he radiated such authority she almost wanted to prostrate herself in front of him and beg forgiveness for some minor and imagined infraction.

'I *will* be the greatest prince Lasserno has ever had. That is how I will be seen. Nothing less will do.'

As she looked into his coldly beautiful face, Hannah had no doubts he'd achieve it. Her only problem was, how on earth was she going to paint it?

* * *

He should have remained seated. He shouldn't be standing anywhere near her, but he was sucked into Hannah's orbit like a galaxy falling to its doom in a black hole. He still couldn't overcome the niggling sensation that he knew her. That alone should have sounded some kind of warning, but he was too enthralled by the way she fought him to worry about a creeping sense of *déjà vu*. Most people bowed or curtseyed. Pandered to his every whim. She didn't seem inclined to do any of those things. She treated him as if he were nobody at all.

It should annoy him, and there was a thread of cool irritation pricking through his veins, but it tangled with something far hotter and more potent. Especially now. When he had last seen her she had been sweetly dishevelled. All mussed up and messy. Somehow completely unattainable because of it. She had looked as if she had no place in his world since there was nothing messy about his life. Not any more. Not since his mother died and he had had to grow up fast, pulling things together because his father had made enough mess for a hundred men.

Yet Hannah today…

Her hair wasn't some tangle of a bird's nest knotted carelessly on top of her head. It swung past her shoulders in a fall of sleek dark chocolate. Soft layers framed her face. Standing this close, he was captivated by her hypnotic green eyes, a wash of deep gold surrounding her pupils, which made them gleam as mysteriously as a cat's. She wasn't paint-spattered, as if that had been some kind of barrier separating them. Her shoes weren't trainers, but polished black knee-high boots which wrapped round her slim calves. Dark jeans hugged her gentle curves. A crisp white shirt was unbuttoned enough to interest, but too high to give anything but a frustrating hint of her cleavage. Somehow, in this moment she looked more woman and less...waif.

What the hell was he doing? It was as if without the paint she'd been stripped of her armour as his artist and become someone attainable. She could never be that. She couldn't be *anything* to him. He was on a quest for his bride, to join him on the throne. A professional matchmaker was putting a list together at this very moment. And now he'd set down that path, his behaviour must be impeccable. No casual liaisons to report to the press in a tell-all that sought to bring him down to his father's level where Alessio would *never* go.

This woman, whilst beautiful and challenging, was effectively his employee. Someone to be afforded appropriate distance and dutiful respect. Not to be the subject of carnal thoughts about her mysterious eyes, or how luscious and kissable her mouth appeared when smoothed with a little gloss...

He stepped away. She'd travelled many hours to be here, and yet he'd brought her to his office and not even offered her refreshments. No doubt she'd need her room and a rest. He'd ask Stefano to take her there and he'd work to regain his equilibrium.

She took a step towards him, hands on her hips. Eyes intent. A picture of defiance. Nothing like the behaviour dictated to her by the dossier he'd asked Stefano to put together, which was as much about his protection as hers.

'If I'm going to paint the *greatest* prince Lasserno has ever had, I need to see where I'm going to work.'

'Of course, follow me.' He said the words without thinking, before his brain engaged to remind him the less time spent in her presence the better. But it didn't matter as his feet carried him towards the door of his office with her following behind. Past Stefano, who simply looked at him with a quizzically raised brow that had become all too familiar since Hannah had entered his life, rose, and followed as well. Against all better judgement, Alessio almost stood him down. Told him to get back to whatever he was doing on his phone and he would handle this, but his better judgement won.

Nowadays, it always did.

'Your home is beautiful,' Hannah said in a breathless kind of voice better suited to quiet, candlelit dinners aimed at seduction than a stroll through the palace halls, but this place inspired similar reactions in those who'd never seen it before. There was nothing special about her.

'Thank you.' He supposed it was the polite thing to say, but he always felt more of a custodian than anything else. It was all a workplace to him. 'My ancestors built it as a fortress in the Renaissance. However, they refused to eschew comfort and style over practicality on the inside. It was designed to intimidate those who sought to intrude, and delight those invited in.'

Which is what the tour guides parroted, through

the public areas. He'd learned their script. It was easier that way, because his view of the place was tainted by the memories of a childhood where even as a young boy he had recognised the chilly dysfunction between his parents, which had soon descended into a fully blown cold war. Before his innocence and any belief his father could be a good man had been shattered for ever in the throne room he would only sit in once, to take the crown. Then he would never enter it again.

'What was it like living here? In all of this? Did you ever break anything precious?'

The only precious thing broken here was trust. 'Never broken anything, no. I was the perfect child.'

'Of course you were. Striding the halls with purpose, even as a ten-year-old.'

No, he'd been playing hide-and-seek with Stefano in places he should not be, when he'd sneaked into the forbidden throne room. Seen his father, with a woman bent over the arm of the throne. Alessio's stride faltered. Hannah almost crashed into him but pulled up close. He knew. He could almost feel her enticing warmth. He turned to the window overlooking a garden.

'I thought you might enjoy the view. Stefano's

ancestors designed the garden in the formal Italian style. I'm sure he'd like to tell you about it.'

Any more quizzical looks from his best friend and Stefano's brows would end with a permanent home in his hairline. Alessio allowed him to tell the story of the famous garden with its clipped hedges and fountains. He stood back, letting the chatter wash over him. Taking slow breaths. *'You will not tell your mother. This is our secret.'* Both his father's cold eyes and the glassy ones of the woman had been on him that day. He could barely understand why his father's hands twisted into her hair as if it had to hurt, though the look on her face spoke nothing of pain, even to his young brain. He hadn't known why their clothes were in disarray, or why his father's free hand had seemed to be in places it shouldn't on a woman, or so he'd thought as a child.

All he knew was that what he was seeing was *wrong.* He'd come to realise later what had been going on in the throne room. How his father had been defiling it. Each day he felt tainted by the creeping guilt at keeping his father's dirty secrets, because the man had made him party to more than one young boy should know. It was as if he'd been trying to mould Alessio into his own, dissolute image to spite his mother.

Lost in his own thoughts, Alessio had failed to realise Stefano and Hannah were now silent.

'Enough of gardens?' he asked, trying to sound suitably composed and regal. He hadn't been assailed by that memory for years and couldn't fathom why it would creep out of its dark, muddy hole to ambush him now.

'It's very beautiful and...ordered.'

'That's the way I like it.' His own thoughts right now were a messy jumble of memories that should never have seen daylight again.

'Do you ever walk in it? Take time to, I don't know, smell the flowers?'

'I... There are no flowers.' Where was all this uncertainty coming from? His role and what was required of him was *all* about certainty. He straightened, remembered exactly who he was. 'As for aimless wandering, I don't have time.'

Stefano had stepped back to his position three paces behind, but Hannah stood right next to him. Looking up with her entrancing green eyes. Lips slightly parted as though there was something always on the tip of her tongue to say.

He had no doubt she'd say it.

'Important prince and all, I know. That's something I need to talk to you about. The time you've allowed for me.'

He'd asked Stefano to schedule the barest minimum for formal sittings. She was following him about like a shadow for the next fourteen days. What more did she need?

'I'm a busy man.'

'Places to be. Country to run. I've seen your diary, but I need more. And I'm talking hours, not minutes.'

They neared the door of her rooms and the adjoining parlour which he had thought would be the perfect place for her to work. Like her studio in England. He'd searched the palace for somewhere with the same alignment. A similar light to fill the room, although here the sun streamed in a bit more brightly than in her own studio. There was no rambling garden outside, but the view was pleasant enough, he supposed. He never really looked any more, too occupied with briefings from his government to gaze at the horizon and contemplate the landscape.

'I can find more, if it's what you require. Perhaps you could accompany His Highness on some…unofficial engagements.' Stefano this time. It was as if both were conspiring against him. 'There's a hospital visit, to see children.'

Those visits were *private*, never made for accolades. 'The children aren't some circus where you watch them perform.'

Hannah frowned. 'I'd never treat sick children that way. But I need to see all aspects of you, not just the official ones. That's what will make my portrait the best.'

Before he could protest, she turned to Stefano and smiled. Wide, warm, generous. The type of smile which sent a lick of heat right to his core. One you could bask in. It had no agenda or artifice at all to add a chill to the edges of it. 'Thank you. Any extra time you can find me would help my work.'

Better her smile be for his friend than him. There was no place for it in his ordered, planned life. One where everything was cool and clinical. That was the way he preferred things to be. Like the hedge garden, clipped and precise. Even though he now felt inclined to take to the palace gym and hit a punching bag, hours earlier than his normal training session, rather than speak to the finance minister about fiscal policy and Lasserno's deficit.

The doors of the room where Hannah would live loomed large. 'Stefano will show you where everything is. I'll leave you to him.'

A gracious host would escort his personal guest in, ensure she was settled. That she was happy with everything, so she'd gift him some genuine smiles which chased away the cold. Instead Alessio strode down the corridor away from Stefano and Hannah, protocol and graciousness be damned. The temptation snapped at him like a whip and he never gave in to temptation.

Smiles like Hannah's were dangerous, because they chased away common sense.

CHAPTER THREE

HANNAH STOOD IN what was best described as an expansive parlour, in the suite of her rooms. It was if she had been dropped into a fairy tale, except she didn't feel like a princess, but an impostor.

Everything here was too magnificent to touch. Her canopied bed with its silks and embroidery in the palest cerulean blues. Magnificent tapestries of pastoral scenes with shepherdesses and frolicking lambs adorning the golden walls. The deepest of carpets she stood on and wiggled her toes into, as if she were walking on a cloud. It reminded her of how threadbare her life back in England seemed to have become, because there was never a time here that anything would be hard or cold. In this palace, nothing would deign to be anything other than perfect. As perfect as the man who ruled here.

The man she was now waiting for, because her equipment had been unpacked and set up in this room to catch the best light. She'd only brought the bare necessities to Lasserno, pencils and charcoal so she could study and sketch, learn about the Prince who would be taking up her next few months of waking thought. She'd set up what she needed on a small side table next to a chair, ready for when His Highness deigned to grace her with his lofty presence.

A sickening knot tightened in her stomach. As if she needed to run rather than be faced with a blank canvas, her empty sketchbook. Hannah ground her teeth against the rising queasiness. She usually loved the challenge of getting to know a new subject. Finding the key to a person, the one that unlocked every brushstroke she'd put down in the time it took to perfect the essence of them on a canvas. But a lot was riding on this commission. Her future. Her home. It wasn't that she was afraid of doing a job she knew so well, afraid of the thrill of knowing a person, of finding the man Alessio hid. Not at all. It was what she stood to lose if she couldn't fulfil it.

She checked the time on her phone. For a man who wanted his portrait painted, he really didn't want to spend much time anywhere near her. Most people enjoyed their sessions, or so she'd been told. She did. She loved learning someone's nuances, the privilege of being allowed to glimpse a private part of a person that many never saw. Alessio seemed to think she could paint him from memory alone. He probably believed that he was unforgettable, so one glance would be all she needed.

He might not be entirely wrong about that.

Enough. She grabbed her sketch pad and watercolour pencils. There was a pretty desk with a view from large windows, overlooking fields of grapes and olives out towards Lasserno's capital. In a copse of ancient olives there peeked a small, domed structure. Like a chapel, or perhaps a folly, although Hannah didn't think Alessio would allow anything so whimsical as that on the palace grounds. The whole scene shimmered with the warmth of a Mediterranean summer. She sat at the fragile-looking desk and sketched, losing herself in perfecting the cobalt blue of the sky, the ochres, umbers and greens of the landscape glowing in the sunshine.

The muffled noise of a well-oiled door handle and hinges made her turn, spring from her chair as if the seat burned her.

Alessio strode into the room, all of him pressed

into hard lines with a flawlessly cut suit and pristine white shirt. A tie of carmine sat at his throat with its fat knot, looking tight enough to strangle. Except she was the one who couldn't get any air, as if he'd sucked it all from the room. He glanced at the gleaming gold watch at his wrist then to her as she wobbled in an uncertain half-dip because she wasn't sure of the protocol if she was going to see him multiple times a day. He flicked his hand in a dismissive kind of way.

'No curtseying unless we are in public.'

'We sort of are, since your secretary's here.' She gave Stefano a little wave. He smiled back in his own handsome kind of way, though it was nothing like the glowering magnificence of his imposing boss.

Alessio looked at her, then to Stefano, and his eyes narrowed. 'You don't strike me as someone who's obtuse, Signorina Barrington.'

'I'm not. You're the one who sent me a volume of rules to follow.'

'So you're prepared.'

'They make me nervous I'm going to get something wrong.' Everything about this made her nervous, particularly him. It was as if all common sense and the need for self-preservation fled in his presence. 'I'm painting your portrait, not stepping out as your significant other. Will you give your princess the same sort of list?'

'No, because, being a princess, she'll know the rules already.'

'Rigidity and protocol don't fit in well with my work. How about we throw away the rules when we're in here?'

He raised one dark, imperious brow. Tugged at the cuffs of his shirt. Checked the time again.

'Who am I to stop you, since it appears you already have?' Alessio stalked towards her where she stood frozen in front of the spindly, gilded desk. She had that sensation again, that she was an insect under a magnifying glass. Alessio loomed close. He wasn't threatening at all. It's that he had a presence. An aura that crammed the space full, till there was no room for anything else. Especially not sensible thought.

'What are you doing there?' He motioned over the sketch she'd started, of the view outside.

'In nine years I've barely gone a day without my art.' There'd been only a few. The anniversaries, where sometimes the grief would steal upon her with a more vicious attack than usual. Sapping her will to do anything but curl up in bed and weep. 'In the last week, I've missed three with all the planning and preparing and I needed to *do* something. It helps me—'

'Relax. I'm like it with horse-riding, yet I rarely get a chance any more.' She froze. The freedom of the ride. Soaring over the jumps in partnership with her horse. She used to revel in that joy too, until the day it represented everything she'd lost. She hadn't ridden since.

Alessio wasn't looking at her unfinished artwork right now, but out of the window, his eyes distant and unfocused. That small offering of something private about himself was a gift and she doubted he realised he'd given it to her. Then the distance in his eyes faded, and they narrowed. As if he'd come back to himself, was pulling himself into reality rather than some faded memories. The whole of him stiffened, and he became the ruler of Lasserno again, rather than a simple man.

'You're drawing with coloured pencils? It seems beneath your reported talents.'

She let out a slow breath, the precious moment lost. 'I use these because they're a challenge for me. Watch.'

She dipped a brush into a small glass of water

which was probably crystal and not designed for this task. Alessio didn't seem to mind. He'd probably drunk from crystal since birth. Nothing as common as plain glass would deign to touch his perfect lips. She took the brush and swiped it gently over a part of the sketched scene. The pencil bled to paint in a wash of colour.

'Magic,' he said.

'Oil paints are forgiving. These, not so much. They're unpredictable, and it's harder to cover up your mistakes.'

'Like life,' Alessio murmured, or at least that was what she thought he said as he moved closer, leaning over the picture. She was sure there was something in that fat instruction booklet about not standing too near him, but for the life of her she couldn't remember what it might have said. Not with all the *proximity*. His height, his magnetic presence. The teasing scent of him, something masculine and fresh like the aftermath of a summer's storm. The warmth he radiated, almost better than morning sunshine. She wanted to lean into it and bask. But she was here to do a job. Having poetic thoughts about unattainable princes was not part of it.

She stood back. Put a respectable distance between them. Likewise, he seemed to shake himself out of the fascination for her simple artwork. He straightened, adjusted his tie. Checked his watch *again.*

'I have limited time. We should start. What do you need from me?'

She needed him to stop being so…him. Instead she pointed to a chair she'd manhandled into better light. He looked at it, at the scuffed carpet where she'd half dragged it across the room. Frowned, but said nothing, instead unbuttoning his jacket and lowering himself into the armchair. Watching her as his secretary watched them both.

'I need fewer people in the room. I can't concentrate like this.'

There were too many eyes on her. She took a slow breath to try and ease the weight of expectation in their stares.

'Stefano stays.'

So imperious. Hannah blew out a huff of breath, grabbed a fresh sketch pad and some sharp-as-a-needle pencils, then sat opposite him. His rich brown eyes fixed on her. There was something addictive about all that focus, as if she were the only person on earth.

Yet even though he sat in a comfortable armchair, he didn't look comfortable. There was nothing relaxed about him, as if he were on edge. *Waiting* for something to happen. Which seemed strange because the man ruled a country. She assumed anything that happened to him was entirely his choice and at his whim. Yet, for all the breathtaking perfection of him, he was still a human and she reminded herself that not all the people she painted were relaxed in the beginning.

'Today, I'll be doing a few sketches. All for reference.' He nodded as she opened her sketchbook. Alessio sat upright, not even his legs crossed. Impossibly formal. She didn't want to focus on his face, nor on those eyes which seemed to barely blink. The rest of him was stitched tight into his suit. But his hands… Veins and tendons corded under his golden skin.

She began to lightly sketch the shape. The elegant, blunt-cut nails. Ignored the slight dusting of dark hair over his metacarpals, hinting around the wrist from under the pure and flawless white cuffs of his shirt. She'd leave those details till later, but for now she marvelled in his long, strong fingers, curled tight over the arms of the chair.

'What have you been doing today?' she asked. The sun streamed through the mullioned windows, brightening the room. A light breeze drifted through one she'd opened earlier.

His jaw tightened. 'Ruling my country.'

'And that involves?'

'Making many important decisions.'

Which was no kind of answer at all. She snorted, looked up at him. His fingers flexed a little. Relaxed, but still not enough. 'Okay, you've been very…princely. Let's take a step back. What time did you get out of bed?'

'Four.'

'A morning person, then.'

His eyes narrowed the merest fraction. 'I'm a busy person.'

'No rest for the wicked?'

A muscle in his strong, square jaw ticked. 'You'll have to ask my father about that maxim.'

She hesitated for a second, the pencil no longer slipping so easily over the paper. When researching Alessio, as she did with every client, she'd read about his father. The man who'd abdicated under the cloud of some scandal. It was all a bit murky. As for the man in front of her, apart from his official website and carefully curated online presence, there was really nothing. Alessio Arcuri presented to the world like the perfect prince.

The press wondered whether Alessio was like his father, and only hid it better.

'Can you take a deep breath in and let it out slowly?'

The tips of Alessio's fingers seemed a little whiter on the arms of the chair, his fingertips denting the fine fabric.

'I don't know what you're asking of me.'

'You seem a bit…' she waved her left hand with the pencil in it, as if drawing in thin air '…rigid.'

'Signorina Barrington, I learned protocol and deportment in classes from the time I could speak.'

He leaned forward, his voice low and cool. Eyes flashing tiger-gold in something like a warning. His forearms now resting on his knees, hands in front. Such a compelling picture. She held her breath and waited for more.

'From the age of five, I could sit perfectly still and silent for well over an hour. Never once moving. If I did move, my tutor's dog had a habit of nipping my ankles. I didn't like getting bitten. So this is how I sit.'

She started another sketch of his hands now, with fingers clasped before him as if in some kind of fervent prayer.

'You can't position yourself like that all the time. What about when you're relaxing? Men, they slouch in a…manly kind of way. Lounging with intent.'

Not that she really had much experience in the way men sat, other than those whose portraits she'd painted, but at least they'd looked at home in the chair she'd placed them in. Alessio's secretary seemed to have relaxation down to an art, having perfected a kind of indolence in the back corner of the room. Or her father, who had always looked comfortable in front of the television with her mother, holding hands. She blinked away the tears her memory wrought. All she knew was that the Prince before her looked as if he were about to order someone's execution.

Perhaps her own. He raised a supercilious brow, his normally full and transfixing lips now a tight line. 'Are you accusing me of not being *masculine* enough?'

'No.' Not a single woman on the planet could ever accuse him of that. She stared at the dark shading of stubble on his jaw, even though it was mid-morning and he must have shaved, at the broadness of his shoulders, the narrow taper of his waist. She was almost suffocated by how masculine he was. All that testosterone made her quite giddy. 'You're the epitome of masculinity. That suit. The bold red tie saying *leader*. Does your valet choose the colour based on what duties you have to attend to? Red for ruling, blue for official visits, yellow for meeting children...'

'Now you're questioning my sartorial choices? What makes you assume I keep a valet?'

'I'm sure all princes have them. To...darn your socks if they get holes in?'

'My socks do not require darning.'

'No, they're probably woven from magical thread by some goddess. I imagine that's your style, impeccable as it is.'

Behind Alessio, his secretary jumped from his chair. He might have looked stricken, but instead he appeared to be choking.

Alessio stood too, and she was forced to look up at his imposing form, the energy around him almost palpable. Not so impassive now, with his jaw hard, nostrils flaring. Even if he wasn't a prince, this man could rule any room he entered.

'Stefano. Please attend the oracle and request the goddess weave me more socks whilst I deal with Signorina Barrington's mocking of me.'

'Any particular colour, Your Highness?'

'Black.' He turned and speared Hannah with a hot glare. 'The colour of my righteous anger.'

Alessio began to pace, something blazing and unfamiliar bubbling in his chest. After years of attempting to inject calm and order into the palace and his life, this woman seemed intent on destroying it in the space of a day. He could not allow anyone to witness it, sending Stefano away before the man fell about laughing, which would have led to jokes at his expense for weeks.

'Alizarin Crimson,' Hannah said.

'What?' He didn't understand her, not at all.

'That would be the colour of righteous anger. It's a deeper colour than simple red...solid, less flash. Now, if you were plain angry, the light version of cadmium red would suit better. So I suggest you should have sent Stefano for red socks rather than black.'

Alessio kept up his pacing, unable to sit still.

No one questioned him any more, no one mocked him, or disagreed with what he said. After years of chaos in the palace, his rule was absolute. That was by his design, and his demand. People knew what he expected of them and complied. No arguments. Gone was the frustration at ideas cast aside, attempts to thwart his father ignored by those who sought to profit from Lasserno's losses. Graft, corruption and sheer negligence had been rooted out ruthlessly. Stefano argued he should release the reins, relax a little. Allow people to see the man rather than the Crown Prince. But that was the way to chaos, no matter what the press made up about him. The standards he set were highest for himself. His recent life was about calm and control. This? Hannah Barrington seemed designed to torment him.

'I don't want to speak about socks. What's the point of these ridiculous questions?'

All the while she'd sat there in her own chair. Wearing black leggings, and some kind of soft grey top which clung to her slender form, sheer enough so he could see the trace of a bra. No colour on her, yet she was the most vibrant thing in the room, and he couldn't look away. Right now she wasn't looking at him, instead gently sweeping an infernal pencil over the page as he wore a path through the carpet, burning through his frustration. She didn't seem to notice. Nibbling on her plum-coloured bottom lip. A slight frown on her brow. Such focus on a piece of paper, not on him.

'I'm trying to engage in conversation,' she said, 'which would be easier if you participated by conversing back.'

'I am speaking to you.'

She glanced up at him briefly, her gaze searching. Flickering over him as if in a quick and efficient study, then back down at the page in front of her. 'Conversation is a different thing entirely. It's an exchange. You're not exchanging, you're… dictating.'

He stopped behind the armchair in which she'd placed him. Gripped the back till his fingers crushed the exquisite fabric. He'd not sat all day, but had been solving a thousand small problems, and a few large ones, on the move. Reviewed the longlist of candidates for Lasserno's new princess. Whilst he'd wished to be anywhere but here, the thought of stopping for the brief hour he'd allocated to her today had been almost pleasant. Yet she'd kept talking, and those questions had dredged up memories and feelings he hadn't experienced in years. It was as though, if he let her speak any more, he might tell her everything that had plagued him since his mother's death.

'So you converse by asking about a valet? What other staff will you be enquiring about? Whether I have my own personal fingernail-buffer?'

He couldn't see what she was doing, the book in which she drew tilted the wrong way. She looked up again from her page. Cocked her head. Fixed her attention to his hands again. Her lips parted, then she went back to drawing.

'That *would* tell me a lot about you, but you strike me as...assured rather than vain.'

He couldn't help a bitter laugh. At least there he hadn't taken after his father. A man always seeking approval, adoration. Being feted for his looks. Searching out women to worship him. His wife's love had never been enough. In the end coldness and hatred was all that had fuelled their doomed marriage.

'So long as my suits fit, I have little interest. I don't need to appear on best-dressed lists year after year.' Unlike his father, who'd eschewed the court-appointed royal tailor for Savile Row. Almost putting the man and his family out of business, when they'd tended royalty in Lasserno for over a century. Alessio had rectified that slight, supporting locals who had a long and proud tradition rather than looking outside the country for what was easily supplied here.

Anyhow, what did a suit matter when all he wanted to do was spend the limited time available to him on horseback, as if to outride the weight of responsibility that some days seemed as if it could crush him? His suit was a mere costume he wore, the trappings of a leader. It said nothing about the man at all.

Hannah stopped drawing, looked at him again. Long, slow. Her gaze drifting over his face, lower. To his hands. Fixing itself there. The way she studied him took on a life of its own. His heart beat a little faster. An odd sensation stirring in his gut, almost like excitement. He released his grip on the chair in front of him and stood straighter. Was her assessment of him an artist's, or a woman's? Did she like what she saw? He didn't know why that last question was so important to answer, because the answer was meaningless and changed nothing.

'Your suit fits...exquisitely.' Her voice was soft, breathy, almost as if what she said surprised her. The tone of it stroked over his skin, touching him everywhere. Alessio relished the sensation. It was like being handed an unexpected gift.

Hannah placed her sketch pad and pencil face down on the carpet. Stood, pursed her lips. 'And I think that's half the problem. Let's start again. Your Highness, could you please take off your suit jacket and have a seat?'

Your Highness. Said with her perfect rounded vowels. A slight huskiness to it. He hesitated, almost as if being asked to remove his jacket were stripping him naked. As she waited for him she tucked an unruly strand of dark hair, that had escaped her efforts to secure it, behind her ear. Alessio peeled the jacket from his body, the air of the room cooling him as he did.

Hannah walked towards him, left hand outstretched. He handed her his jacket. She took it and hung it over the back of a small dining chair, running her hands over the shoulders. A stunning flash of heat tore through him as he imagined those hands stroking over his own shoulders. Something that could never, ever happen. He sat in the armchair again. Settling in to get comfortable when all of him was on edge. Tried to *lounge with intent*, whatever that meant.

'You should take off the tie.' Alessio didn't think. He moved his hands to the red silk. Loosened it, and only had a fleeting moment where he could finally breathe before his chest tightened again. He held out his hand with the tie and she took it, the minutest brush of her fingertips on his, and the world could have stopped turning, on the precipice of tempting desires he must ignore.

Was she affected too? Her hands caressed the tie, gently smoothing the fabric, wrapping it round her palm to create a perfect spiral and placing it on a side table. Then she faced him. Perhaps the colour was higher on her cheeks? Or perhaps he was projecting his own torrid desires onto her.

It had been a long time since he'd been with a woman. When he realised the extent of his father's profligate behaviour, he'd seen no choice but for his own to be exemplary. All his waking hours had been taken up with trying to draw attention from his father, hiding his ultimate disgrace, rebuilding Lasserno's reputation. He would not let his people suffer at the hands of his family. These things required him to be better.

He shouldn't crave the softness of a touch. He'd inured himself to such things because of the job he must do. It required toughness, no distractions. He'd risen above it before. He would again.

But how for a few bright, blinding moments did he wish he could fall.

She moved closer again, looking down on him. A strange and discomfiting position to be in. As if for the first time he was at some kind of disadvantage, when his whole life had been full of the advantages of his position. Her eyes were luminous in the late-morning light. A mysterious wash of green and gold, like the ocean close to the shore. Hannah cocked her head. Pointed, waggling her finger at him. He shouldn't have tolerated that. It was a breach of protocol, but protocol be damned. He didn't care.

'The top two buttons as well.'

Dio, in this moment she could have him completely naked if she asked. The thrill of that thought was intoxicating. The whole atmosphere in the room thickened, time slowing to these perfectly innocent words weighted with his illicit imaginings. Alessio didn't even think. He undid the two buttons on his shirt. More slowly than he ought, since she kept her gaze on every move of his fingers, almost as if hoping he didn't stop, that he undid all of them.

Or that was what he imagined. In his fantasies he could allow it. Never in reality.

She moved her hand, as if she were reaching out again. Hesitated. Checking herself. Her lips parted. Then she dropped her arm and stepped back. Shook her head.

'What?' His voice was rough as it ground out of him. Frustrated at the things he could not have.

Hannah went back to her chair. Grabbed her sketch pad and pencil. 'I thought you might run your hands through your hair. Make it a little untidy.'

Their gazes clashed and held. He'd look as if he'd rolled out of bed if he did that. Did she want him messy? As though they'd spent a night together? His hands involuntarily gripped the satiny fabric of the chair again, to hold on to something.

'But then I realise that untidy wouldn't be you... Your Highness.'

He almost shouted to her that yes, it was. He could be that man. He had been in the past, when life had been freer and he'd thought only of riding for his country, not taking the throne too soon and repairing the disaster wrought by his father. But she'd reminded them both, with his title, that he was born to a job and would not deviate. He clenched his teeth. Swallowed down the bitter taint of disappointment as she began her drawing again, with deft moves of her pencil that felt as if she were inscribing on his skin. He wondered what else she saw of him, with her artist's eyes.

'Could you answer a question for me?' she asked. 'One question, honestly, with no equivocation?'

Alessio gritted his teeth. He'd kept so much of himself private for so long, particularly after Allegra's attempts at courting the press, that agreeing to any question he didn't vet beforehand was unnatural to him. Most respectable journalists in Lasserno knew this and played the game with the rules he'd set. The tabloids made up what they wanted in the absence of a story. He didn't like this stranger, this young, almost guileless woman, demanding parts of him he rarely granted to anyone.

'Yes.' She didn't look up. Showed no reaction to his agreement at all. But he wasn't giving away everything without exacting a price. 'So long as you answer one of mine.'

Her head whipped up from the page. She was paying attention to him now, and something hot and potent thrummed through him. He liked it far too much.

'That's not how this works. It's all about you.'

'You want to know so much of others yet give none of yourself.' She nibbled on her bottom lip again, drawing his attention to her distracting mouth. The way her teeth worked on the soft flesh. He craved to soothe away the sting of her teeth, see if her lips were as soft as they looked.

'It's my job.'

'People might accuse you of having something to hide.'

He wasn't sure she had secrets. She'd been investigated before the commission for his portrait was requested. In his life now, that was a given. But in some perverse way he enjoyed her discomfort, since she was causing him so many inconvenient and uncomfortable thoughts of his own.

'I don't have any secrets. I just find people prefer to talk about themselves. I'm not that interesting. But if you answer my question, you can ask one of yours.'

She shrugged, and the soft shirt she wore sagged a little, exposing the hint of a bra strap before she pushed it back onto her shoulder. But he didn't miss the slice of pale blue, and he firmly shut down imaginings of whether her underwear was lace or something practical. Instead, he checked his watch. Their hour had almost ended, and yet he didn't want to leave. How long could he wait here, sitting in the chair, before someone would come to find him?

'Then ask what you wish.'

'If you want to escape from it all, what do you do?'

He could have laughed, the answer so easy it required no effort at all. 'I ride my horses.'

Her look softened a fraction, or perhaps it was his imagination. The corners of her mouth turning up, her gaze seeming far away. It almost appeared wistful, but the moment was lost as she went back to her drawing. He could have asked her any question at all, but that fleeting look on her face spoke to him in some way.

'Do you ride, Signorina Barrington?'

Her pencil dragged to a stop on the page. Her

eyes a little wider as she paled, looking almost…
fearful.

'I—I haven't…not for a long time.'

He wondered whether she would answer more
questions if he asked them, but a respectful
knock sounded at the door. He let out a long,
slow breath. The knock reminded Alessio of his
real life, not the fantasy that he could do what he
wished, without all the responsibilities he had.
He rose from his chair as the door opened and
Stefano walked inside. Holding a pair of black
socks. An eyebrow raised, meaning he would
ask questions about what went on in this room
whilst he was away, which Alessio would not
deign to answer. He needed to go now, but his
decision was simple. She wanted to get to know
the man? He had the perfect answer.

'Prepare yourself. Tomorrow, meet me at the
stables. Then we'll ride.'

CHAPTER FOUR

HANNAH HESITATED AT the door of the magnificent stables on the lower reaches of the palace grounds. Assailed by the earthy scents she'd once loved, of lucerne, hay and straw. In the past that smell had signalled her happiest moments. Spending time with her precious horse, Beau. The hours brushing him, mucking out the stables, never a chore. She'd dreamed of owning stables like this back then. Such fleeting, futile fantasies before everything had turned to dust.

The awe of the space mingled with a heaviness in her chest, making it hard to breathe. She didn't want the memories now. This stable, riding, were symbols of a life lost to her. There was no escaping it here. The glint of crushed metal, the tick of a hot, broken engine. The dread silence from her parents. The terrified whinnies of her mortally injured horse. It all came back with a sickening rush. She faltered for a second. Stood to take it in, work it through. For a moment, the pain of that day was as sharp and bright as if it had just happened. But she had no choice other than to be here. Hannah took a deep breath. This was simply a job. Though it didn't stop the sense of regret and loss almost overwhelming her.

She walked to where she'd been told to go. Where two horses now stood saddled, with a person she assumed was the groom. Their tack was shiny and perfect.

That sick feeling intensified...the roar of blood surging in her ears, her heart pounding against her ribcage. Everything was swirling in a dizzying attack to her senses of a day when life as she knew it had ended. She'd lost her hopes and dreams in the accident. Her whole life had changed. She'd rebuilt it, but some days the foundations seemed a little unstable. As if everything could fall apart again. Which was more truth than a lie, after what her uncle had done. A sense of betrayal sliced through her again, that the people she should have been able to trust had failed her. It all came down to work in the end, yet right now if she could turn around and flee, leave handsome princes and shattered dreams behind, she would. But her choices ended with her uncle's embezzlement. Hannah faltered, stopped for a second. Took some steadying breaths as her legs trembled.

How was she going to get on a horse's back, when she could barely walk to where they stood?

'Signorina Barrington?'

That voice from behind. Deep, with a lilting accent. Smoothing over her like some balm to her troubled soul. The prickling sensation of someone close. Alessio's presence penetrating the cold grief threatening to overwhelm her.

She turned. He crowded out everything else in the space, not as close as she'd thought, but it didn't matter how far away he stood, she was sure she'd still feel him. It was as if he had an aura a mile wide, obliterating her awareness of anything else. And if she'd been faltering before, right now she was paralysed.

She'd glimpsed him a few times at a distance when she'd been competing, dressed for competition himself. He'd been overwhelming then, to a young girl with hormones making themselves known in confusing ways, like a fairy tale brought to life. But nothing prepared her for this, Alessio in a short-sleeved polo shirt which showed off his tanned skin, the swell of his impressive biceps, the strength of his forearms. His legs, encased in buff breeches and riding boots, caused her mouth to dry. Because, whilst all of him was only hinted at under a suit, this figure before her wasn't the young man she'd pined over, whose riding she'd watched obsessively whenever she could find it. He was a thirty-one year old in his prime and it showed in every inch of him. His broad chest, muscular thighs. Which she probably shouldn't be staring at, and...was her mouth open? She closed it. She was only trying to get air, that was all. Trying to stop her heart pounding. But it wasn't the sickening rhythm of before, instead morphing into something harder, more insistent. The drumbeat of a pulse that spoke of a sultry type of rhythm she tried hard to ignore.

As she looked up from how well his breeches fitted and into his face, he frowned, the merest of creases in his otherwise unmarred forehead. Probably judging the worn old jeans she'd sneaked into her bag almost out of spite, because she was sure nothing that much past their prime would ever grace the palace walls.

'Are you all right?' Something about his question made everything inside her still. It was as if he saw her. 'You look pale. You're not afraid of horses, are you?'

She shook her head. The fear was not of the animals, but of the memories. 'No. Probably a little late to sleep, a little early to wake.' It wasn't exactly a lie. The thought of riding with him today had left her tossing and turning, with dreams of running after things she couldn't catch, of accidents she couldn't prevent. 'As I said, I haven't ridden for a while.'

Still, his gaze searched her. As if he realised she wasn't telling the truth. 'Come. Meet your horse. If you have any fears, she should allay them.'

He walked ahead of her, and for once she was happy to follow as his rule book dictated. It was no chore to watch his long, assured stride, taking in her fill of the broad shoulders tapering to his narrow waist. She shouldn't look, really, but what woman wouldn't stare at that backside? Her cheeks burned hot at the prickling awareness of him, and how magnificent he was. They arrived at the groom, and Alessio turned, the corner of his mouth quirking in a smile which told her he *knew* she'd been staring and didn't really mind.

Typical.

He reached out and rubbed the silky nose of an impossibly pretty dapple grey. 'This is Kestia. She's a placid mare who knows what she's doing. You'll have no trouble with her. I promise.' Alessio stared at Hannah as he said it, narrowed his eyes. Cocked his head a fraction.

She didn't like that look. It was as if he was contemplating things he didn't want to say. Hannah narrowed her own eyes back at him.

'You're not thinking that I'm a…troublesome mare, are you?'

His full and perfect mouth curled into something of a wry grin. Her breath caught. When he wasn't so stern and forbidding, he was the type of man who could cleave a woman's heart in two if she allowed it. Which was risky, when there were so few pieces of her heart left to break. Alessio placed a hand flat over his chest. 'I'd never think such a thing.'

She needed a distraction from him so she reached out and stroked down her horse's side with her flat hand. The coat was smooth and warm to the touch. Alessio watched the gentle move, before his umber eyes held her gaze for a heartbeat. Then it was as if he came to himself and stepped back, his face cool and impassive again. He moved to his own horse. A dark bay stallion. Tall. Clipped mane. Gleaming coat. His ears were pricked high and his eyes were alert. Nostrils flaring. The sort of horse she would have given anything to ride.

'He's magnificent,' she said, as Alessio took his mount's reins.

'Apollo's special. However, I've been ignoring him lately and if I don't take him out soon he'll punish me. His groom rides him but for some reason he prefers me. It seems we have an affinity.'

'You're both hot-blooded?' She didn't know where those words had come from. They blurted out of her but both Alessio and his horse seemed tense, as if they were bristling to break into a run and never stop.

'He was inclined in the past to be more reckless than is good for him. He's fearless when sometimes he should be cautious.' Alessio stroked his horse's nose. 'He's settled since I've owned him. Is a champion in all ways.'

Alessio had been fearless too, once. She wondered what had happened to him and his showjumping. The reasons he'd stopped had been lost in the annals of history, the internet only briefly mentioning his riding. It was as though that part of him had been scrubbed away. But she remembered him. He'd left her breathless, even then. She had scoured the internet for videos of his events. Watching him over and over. Why give it all away when he was rising to the top of an elite field with everything ahead of him?

'Would you compete again? With Apollo?'

'I have a country to rule. There is no time for anything else.' Alessio's eyes were bleak and distant. He cleared his throat, nodded to the little grey. 'We should ride. We don't have much time, and a dinner tonight to ready ourselves for.'

The dinner. Of course. Though she wondered how much time he thought she needed to get ready, because it was hours away yet.

They mounted their horses with the assistance of the groom, and she settled herself into the saddle, the warmth of the animal's body seeping into her. Familiar and heartbreaking in so many ways but exhilarating in others. The sensation washed over her again, here, up high. Of being capable of anything. That was how she'd felt once. As if life were full of promise rather than weighed down by reality.

How she wished she could be that sixteen-year-old girl again. To have the freedom and belief that everything would always be okay. To have the hope for life and love, rather than the inevitability that loss was always the risk when you loved another. She had taken years to contemplate dating, at Sue's encouragement. She'd been introduced to someone who might not have made her heart race but seemed kind. Solid and safe. She had thought there was something there, allowed herself the tiniest shred of hope that there was a future worth waiting for. Only to have it crushed when he had said art took up too much of her time. He had wanted some fun, and that it was painting or him. As if she could stop something that was intrinsic to her being. And with his words, any hope had died too. It was an unacceptable risk now. The prickle in her eyes and sting in the back of her nose warned of tears. The grief bubbling close, especially here. Of what she'd lost, sure, but also of what might have been. She took a deep breath, steadied herself. Loosened her grip on the reins and tried to relax a bit.

This fortnight was a job. This moment, a simple ride on a sweet mare with a subject she was supposed to paint. Nothing more. And that subject looked incomparable astride his horse,

Apollo prancing in anticipation of leaving the stables, Alessio's control light, brilliant.

'He's impatient to get going,' she said.

'Always.' Hannah wondered if he was talking about his horse or himself—both looked outside the stable doors as if they wanted to bolt and never return. 'Are you ready?'

She nodded, the unsettled queasiness still rumbling around her stomach. Alessio walked them out of the stables and she rode beside him, the rhythm of it all familiar and as comforting as it was heartbreaking.

'I'm surprised Stefano isn't here with us.'

Alessio snorted and his horse flicked and twisted his ears, as attuned to his rider as his rider was to him. 'You'd never see him on the back of a horse. I think he's afraid of them, but he denies it. Are you comfortable riding faster than a walk? Apollo needs to move.'

She nodded and Alessio nudged his horse into a trot. She followed, settling into the rise and fall of it. She pulled in beside him, keeping up easily. He'd been right. She might be a little rusty, taking a while to learn her horse's stride whereas once it would have almost been instinctive, but she hadn't forgotten, even after all these years.

'Where are we going?' she asked. They curved along a path, the sound of the horses' hooves thumping on the ground in a soothing rhythm. If she had her bearings right, they were riding out into the view she saw from her window each day.

'Through the vines, out past the olive grove, then circling back. It should take about an hour and there's space if you feel confident enough to let the horses gallop.'

She felt almost confident enough now, sitting up on her beautiful grey, feeling that familiar thrum of excitement, the desire to take off and be free. But she didn't want Alessio asking questions about her experience. About why she had stopped riding too. It was so hard to hold back, when all she wanted to do was lose herself in the speed of her mount to feel as if she were flying again.

'From the window of my room there's an interesting little domed building amongst some trees. Can we go and see it?'

She didn't miss the slight tightening of his hands on the reins. The way his horse became restive and tossed his head. Broke his even stride. Alessio murmured softly in Italian. Almost like an apology to Apollo for disturbing him. Then he glanced back at her.

'The pavilion. *Ovviamente*. Of course.'

He led the way past some low fences, towards the grapevines burgeoning with fruit where a few people worked.

'Do you ever jump these?' She nodded to some little gates obstructing the gravel path to the stables. Alessio gave an almost smile. The merest tilt of his lips. Something distant and somehow... wistful.

He turned to her, and her fingers itched for the scratch of pencil on paper, to catch the question in his eyes, the curve of his mouth. The certainty in the way he held himself, that this was his rightful place and destiny. Whilst the idea of a blank canvas had terrified her before, she could see this. How she'd shape the paint to fit him, his body owning the canvas as he owned this land.

'*Sì*. My horses are all able.' The people in the vines ahead of them raised their hands and waved. He waved back. 'I may need to speak to my vigneron later. About the harvest.'

'Everything going well?'

'It looks to be a good vintage. A perfect showpiece for our country's wine industry, and what it can achieve.' He said the words with steel-edged pride, as if it was a personal achievement.

They rode on into the shade of some glorious old olives, gnarled and ancient, the dappled sun warm on her skin, the scent of earth and horse everywhere. She'd forgotten the joy of this, the simple pleasures of riding in nature.

'The countryside is beautiful here,' she said. 'I'm surprised Lasserno's not more popular. There isn't much advertising about its tourism.'

His shoulders stiffened. 'It's a hidden treasure but people think we're a poor cousin of Italy, no matter the natural beauty and riches. We've been undervalued for too long, not enough made of our assets. Industries like winemaking have been left to crumble and waste away. I sought to change that the minute my father left the throne.'

'Was he keen to retire?'

'The only thing he was keen to do was plunder the country's riches for himself. People suffered…the treasury was emptied. I feared nothing would be safe.' Alessio's jaw clenched. 'Had he not abdicated the role I would have taken it from him.'

Even though the temperature was warm, the breeze cool, it was as if she'd been plunged into midwinter. She didn't know what to say. Alessio talked about making war with his own father, and that added another layer to the complex picture he painted for her. This man was the one you'd commit to canvas wielding a sword on horseback, like the imposing portraits of his ancestors.

They rode in silence for a little longer. It was as if he'd said too much and she guessed he had, being normally so self-possessed.

'Are we going to the pavilion?'

He turned to her, his eyes bleak and cold. 'You still wish to see it?'

She nodded. Anything to break the terrible chill that had fallen over them. His shoulders slumped a fraction, and it seemed almost like a defeat. Then he straightened again as if steeling himself.

'Come this way.'

Alessio wheeled his horse around and encouraged him into a canter, as if he'd forgotten she hadn't ridden for years. And all she could do was try to follow in his wake.

Alessio didn't know what it was about Hannah, how when she asked a question it was as if he'd been injected with a truth serum. He said what he wanted, what he'd bottled up, like purging his soul. In that way she was dangerous, non-disclosure agreement aside. People might have tried guessing things about his father, the reasons why he had stepped down, but the truth had been well hidden. Alessio had ensured it. Lasserno's former prince had been all about laziness and destruction. However, *no one* should ever know the extent to which Alessio had investigated removing him. Perhaps his father had had an inkling before his abdication. The palace had been full of spies and sycophants before Alessio had rid the place of them. That could be why his father had jumped before being given an unceremonious push, because Alessio had been ready to give him a final shove if it meant saving the country.

But this was a secret the world could never know, because it signalled instability. Let everyone believe the lie his father had done it for the good of the country. Yet today Alessio had put everything at risk, all because of the gentle questions of the woman riding with him.

Hannah followed close behind him as they approached the pavilion. He wasn't surprised she'd asked to see it, such a quaint building peeking out of the olive grove. A folly to something that would never last. He wondered what Hannah would see here. Whether she'd sense the tragedy or only see the fantasy of the place. Alessio wasn't sure why her opinion on these things mattered.

He pulled up Apollo and dismounted, the curdle of dread filling his stomach. Here sat a tribute by his mother to a love that had burned brightly and exploded in a supernova-like cataclysm, before imploding into darkness, cold and endless. So many hopes and dreams had been built into this little structure. A testament to the dismal failure of relationships. His father, unwilling to be faithful. His mother, unable to forgive. Their country the ultimate loser. Alessio curled his loose reins around an ancient olive tree. Hannah dismounted with a practised ease that belied her supposed inexperience and did the same, her boots crunching in the fallen leaves on the ground as she approached him.

'This is such a beautiful spot.' Her voice was a little breathy as she looked around, her cheeks with a healthy pink glow.

Yes, it was a pretty spot in the dappled sunshine. The whitewashed pavilion with a domed terracotta roof tucked away in the shade. But it had nothing on her. In her worn jeans and buttoned shirt which clung to her elegant curves she glowed as if from the inside out, with something that looked a lot like joy.

'Can we go inside?'

He nodded. 'It's never locked.'

He walked up some small stairs, turned a latch and entered the place he hadn't visited in years. Not since the death of his mother when he had come here and raged at the universe for stealing the wrong parent. But demons needed to be conquered, especially for him now the country was his to rule. There was no place he could fear to tread, not now.

The pavilion had been kept pristine. No leaf or dust dared grace any surface. The floor was an exquisite mosaic of the goddess Venus rising from the waves. Fluted columns against the walls supported the roof, decorated in between with leadlight windows and pantheons of gods staring down at them. A few wooden benches sat inside. Once they'd been covered with plush cushions, this structure designed as an opulent meeting place, away from the strictures and rules of the palace.

Hannah followed him inside, stood in the middle of the room looking up at the ceiling with the painted plaster like a summer's sky. She turned on the spot, her lips parted, face alive as if in wonder.

'What is this place used for? The light's gorgeous. It would be a beautiful space to paint in.'

Alessio shrugged. 'Nothing now. Once it was a retreat. A place to be alone. To contemplate.'

The lies…all the lies. They threatened to choke him even though they needed to be told. He wouldn't betray his mother's memory at the way his parents had debased themselves in their horror of a marriage towards the end.

'It seems almost like it was built for… I don't know. Lovers.'

So close to the truth, this woman. Always probing and finding the right answers. She could be a danger to his equilibrium if he didn't proceed with care.

'It was built by my mother on the second anniversary of her marriage, as a gift to my father.'

'That's so romantic.' Her voice was the merest whisper, the brush of a cool breeze through the olive trees surrounding them.

'Yes, isn't it? Romance is all around us.' His

voice in response sounded hard, cynical. Even to his own ears. Echoing in this little space with nothing soft to absorb it.

In truth, this building was a testament to a failed marriage. His parents' relationship had been reported as one of great passion, until his father became bored after Alessio was born. This building hinted at something grand and consuming. Love perhaps. Obsession more likely. Or a desperate, clinging hope of keeping something that was already slipping away. He had no memory of his parents' love, only what cold, black coals were left when the flame had burned out.

'You say that like romance isn't a good thing.'

A slight frown marred her brow, those eyes of hers watching him. Assessing all the time. The sense of it prickled down his spine. A warning that he was transparent as glass and she could see all his cracks and flaws underneath. She was an artist after all. She was programmed to look for those things. He didn't want her to see them. They were secrets he kept from the world. The face he projected was the one he wanted her to paint, not the man he hid.

'If not reciprocated, it's a disaster.' The shouts, the fights. The priceless porcelain hurled across rooms, smashing against walls. His mother's cry. *'You loved me once!'* His father's reply. *'I hate you now.'* That was where romance ended. In rage and recrimination.

'What about you?' he asked. 'Would you build such a lofty monument to romance yourself?'

Hannah looked around the space. Tucked an unruly strand of hair behind her ear. She nibbled at her plump, peach lips. But she wouldn't look at him.

'My art takes up all of my time and emotion.' She appeared to have hunched in on herself, as if she were trying to tuck herself in, fold herself away till she was hidden. 'And that's enough.'

He understood his own attitude all too well. Love was a lie. Romance a folly as real and palpable as the building in which they stood. He wondered what led a young woman like her to reject it, when most had their heads in the clouds.

'So cynical for one so young,' he murmured. And something of a kindred spirit, but he didn't want to think of that. Of the way she stood there. Her cheeks coloured a beautiful pink from the warmth of the day and the mild exertion. How her eyes were the translucent green of Lasserno's coastline, where the water met the rocky shore.

How they were alone, where the only thing he could hear were the birds and the whisper of a summer's breeze through the trees outside. The beat of his heart thudding in his ears. Then she looked up at him, a flash in her eyes like sun on the sea. Her gaze casting down his body, then back to meet his. Her lips parted.

This, between them, was nothing about romance but something more primal—though no less destructive. An awareness like a match freshly struck and flaring to life. If he were another man he would have taken the few steps forward to close the space between them, wrapped her in his arms, kissed her and explored this attraction. The heat of desire coursed through his veins, settled down low. Snapping at his heels to prompt him into action. He took a deep breath against the immediacy of this craving. Something he didn't want or need.

The only thing he had to rule his life by was the desire to serve his country. To be better. The best. And nothing else would do, particularly not following this desire running between them when nothing could ever come of it.

'We should move on,' he said. 'The horses need

exercise. But if the light appeals, you may come here and paint.'

At least it might help keep her away from him and his incendiary desires with no outlet.

'Thank you.' Hannah's voice was low and husky, the sensation of it scoring over his skin.

They left the small pavilion and he shut the door behind them, on the past. He was all for moving forward, the only direction for him now. They approached the horses, happily nibbling on some grass under the trees, heads lifting and ears pricking as they approached.

'I'll give you assistance to mount Kestia.' He didn't want his horse's back hurt by an inexperienced rider struggling to get on. It had nothing to do with a need to move close, where he could smell the scent of her like the apple trees which graced the sheltered orchards of the palace gardens. It most certainly was not an excuse to touch Hannah in any way, to feel the warmth of her body through her jeans as he assisted her onto the horse, but he needn't have worried. She was graceful, assured. Almost as if she'd been born in the saddle on which she sat. Looking perfect on the horse he'd bought for his future princess, whoever she might ultimately be from the list of candidates now sitting in the top drawer of his desk. After Hannah left, after his coronation, then he'd decide that part of his future. He still had time.

Alessio shoved those thoughts aside. He swung himself onto Apollo's back and led through the olives into the heat of the day, pointing out landmarks as he saw them. Anything to keep his mind off the way her cheeks glowed pink in the warm sunshine, the way soft strands of her dark brown hair escaped the riding helmet, curling round the base of her neck.

He'd rather encourage Apollo into a gallop and keep riding till both were exhausted and covered in sweat, to burn away these sensations that were so foreign to him. And he couldn't sit here any longer, taking this sedate pace. He needed more, to outrun the crushing in his chest. The feeling of being trapped in a way he couldn't explain.

Reprieve came from a man walking through the grapevines in the distance.

'Do you feel confident enough to ride back to the stables yourself? As I said, I need to speak with my vigneron.' It wasn't far and Kestia was quiet and sound.

Hannah hesitated for a second, then nodded. 'I'll be fine. You go ahead.'

It didn't take a moment to encourage Apollo to move. Alessio clicked his tongue and the horse knew what he wanted, accelerating into a gallop and giving them both the freedom they craved.

Hannah watched Alessio ride out. The magnificence of it as he took off over the landscape. She settled Kestia, the little horse becoming impatient seeing the big bay streak away into the distance. Hannah patted her neck as they walked a short way. Out of Alessio's presence it was almost as if she could let out a long-held breath, those moments in the pavilion, built as a tribute to love and romance, filling her with something she barely understood. An awareness that took root and grew unchecked and uncontrolled in that little space, and for the briefest, blinding flash she craved to explore it for herself. But those feelings led nowhere. They were remnants of childish fantasies and nothing more.

Now she was firmly grounded in reality, sitting on the back of a beautiful horse for the first time in nine years. That was a thrill of its own, and with Alessio occupied she could ride as she wanted with no one to ask questions of her.

'Okay, little girl, let's see what you can do.' She encouraged her horse into a trot through the vibrant landscape, the sun high in a cobalt sky, a cool breeze making the afternoon comfortably warm rather than oppressive. They broke out onto the path, towards the castle rising majestically from the landscape. Like a fantasy picture made real.

She spurred her horse on a little faster now, settling into the rhythm, the quiver in her belly all about excitement. How had she forgotten how alive this made her feel? It was as if a switch had been flicked, a light turned on, illuminating all the dark and missing corners in her life. Ahead lay the low gate they'd passed on the way out on their ride and Kestia's ears pricked. Hannah's heart thrummed in her chest, the excited beat of it because this jump was *easy* and she was going to take it. As they approached the obstacle Hannah checked the length of her mount's stride, preparing them for the jump. Adjusted her position and they flew, for the briefest of moments, before safely landing on the other side.

All those things she'd suppressed, forced herself to forget, coalesced into that bright, brilliant moment soaring over the fence. The jump hadn't been difficult for either of them, but still she patted her little horse, whispered words of praise as the tears stung in her eyes. The memories of competition, her parents' pride at her success… There was joy in this moment, but it was also suffused with a deep ache which never really went away.

She rode on, not slowing her horse. They entered the stable area and she dismounted with a smile which might not leave her for hours, rubbing Kestia's mane, smoothing her hands over her soft coat. The thud of hooves in the distance caught her attention and she glanced outside to see Alessio galloping towards them like a warrior. He rode into the stables with a flash and clatter of hooves and pulled up his horse, leaping from Apollo and stalking towards her, reins in hand.

'What the hell do you think you were doing?' His eyes glittered like black diamonds. Jaw clenched hard enough to shatter teeth.

'Riding?' She stroked her horse's velvety nose, trying to ignore the man crackling next to her with the energy of a summer storm. 'She's wonderful. A dream.'

'As she should be,' he hissed, his breathing hard from exertion. 'You could have hurt her by pulling a stunt like that!'

Hannah refused to accept the approbation. She might do many things, but she'd never hurt a horse. 'It was no stunt. I—'

'You said you couldn't ride!'

'I said I hadn't ridden in a long time.' Hannah glared at him, the excitement of the ride still coursing rich and hot through her veins. She stood straight and tall, holding her ground, hands planted on her hips, not caring if this broke every rule in his stupid handbook. Alessio didn't move, vibrating with a furious energy. It was as if both of them were sizing up the other for a fight. She took off her riding helmet and scrubbed her hands through her hair, damp with sweat. 'You told me she could jump and the quality of your horses is obvious. I would *never* have done anything beyond her capabilities. It's not as if I hopped on her back and threw her straight over the fence. We've ridden for an hour already. I had her measure.'

His sensual lips thinned. The merest of frowns

creased his brow. 'You've been holding back on me. All morning.'

Something of a warning flashed in his eyes and she knew it was because she hadn't admitted the truth to him earlier in the day. And that was a problem because he'd been holding back for her too, when they both could have ridden like the wind together. But she hadn't wanted him to ask questions about her skills, rusty as they were in the beginning. Questions led to conversations, and conversations brought back memories now bubbling close to the surface, of things which had haunted too many of her days, and some of her nights even still.

'I said I thought we'd met—'

'We haven't…as adults.'

That was why she and her friend had been in the car together and she hadn't travelled with her parents. They'd been giggling and gossiping about *him*.

'I've seen you ride before. I recognise your style and I'll always remember a horse. Who was yours?'

It wasn't really a question but a command. He stood there formidable, with the assurance of a person to whom no one would say no. The type of person who was never unsure. She'd remembered him like that, when she was only sixteen and unsure about everything. His confidence, the certainty about him. Part of her wanted to knock him down now, refuse to answer his questions. But she'd be damned if he thought she'd be reckless on horseback. All she needed to do was withstand the memories that would once again storm over her, leaving her wrung out for days. She couldn't do that here. There was nowhere to shut herself away and grieve unrestricted.

'His name was Beauchamp... Beau.'

'A palomino?'

She nodded, astounded Alessio could remember. Beau was so beautiful he had looked as if he'd been forged from gold. She might have had no siblings, but he was like her brother, her best friend. His loss in such a terrible way, with her parents, had almost broken her. He might have survived the accident, but he hadn't been able to survive the mortal injuries. She'd wanted everyone to try, because he was all she had left after her parents had died instantly, but the vet said no, and in the end others had made the decision she couldn't make for herself. She'd never shaken the feeling she'd let them both down that day, and in those moments any sliver of hope something might be left to her out of the horror had died with him.

She turned her head, not wanting Alessio to see the vulnerability, the tears that she couldn't prevent.

'You were good. You could make him fly like you both had wings.' Hannah couldn't believe Alessio had noticed her, could remember her horse. She'd always thought he was the type of man who wouldn't notice anyone like her.

'Why did you stop?' he asked.

She couldn't answer that question, not now. 'Why did you?'

Her voice threatened to crack. She reined in the emotion.

'Always with the questions, yet no answers for me,' he said. 'How does someone so young have so much to hide?'

She shrugged. 'I could ask the same.'

He hesitated for a second, which was pronounced because he was a man who hesitated at nothing. 'My country needed me. And you?'

The desire to say it was like a poisoned thing bursting out of her chest and she couldn't contain it any longer.

'There was an accident. My parents. My horse. I lost everything.' Hannah let out a long, slow breath. Closed her eyes. Rested her forehead on Kestia's warm body.

'When I left England, my groom told me of a tragedy but there were few details. I had no idea it was you.' His voice was soft and kind, but it didn't really help. Nothing did. 'I'm sorry.'

'It was a long time ago now, and it's fine. Really.'

Those were the lies she told herself. So many lies. She'd wondered for years what was the purpose of her surviving, till she found she could document the moments of others so precious memories would never be lost. That was her calling now. Photos might fade, but she tried to paint those portraits capturing an essence a photo never could. Her pictures could hang on a wall, there for ever.

'No. It's not.' A brush of heat coursed through her from the soft touch of Alessio's fingers at her elbow. The gentle pressure somehow comforting. She turned around, looked into his darkly handsome face. The tightness of his eyes, the pinch to his mouth. Pain drawn across him, reflecting her own. 'I was called home after my mother fell ill. Then we lost her. The country might have shared the grief but in truth it was all mine, and nothing about that is fine, Hannah. It is as if nothing will ever be fine again.'

He'd moved forward. They stood so close now, the heat from his body warming her cold soul. She wanted to take it all for herself. Wrap herself in it like a blanket and let him comfort her for ever, because in some small way he understood.

'There were days when it was all too hard.'

'And yet here we are today.'

Their bodies were hidden behind the horses, where no one could see. She was so aware of the solidity of him, his broad shoulders holding the weight of grief. The burdens of a prince. How she wished some days she could share hers with another, let them carry the load for a while. Let someone with the strength of this man shoulder them. But that was a vulnerability she couldn't afford because it wouldn't last, a gateway to more pain, and she'd had enough in her twenty-five years to last her a lifetime.

Yet the moment seemed full, teeming with things unsaid, emotions repressed waiting to explode. Hovering between everything, and nothing at all. She could smell him this close, the seaside tang of fresh male sweat from their ride in the sun, and the undertone of something else dark and sweet like treacle she could drown in. One step closer and they'd touch. That was all it would take, a move from either of them.

Alessio cupped her cheek, his palm burning on her flesh. The look in his eyes soft. Sad, as if carrying the weight of the world. Then he slid his hand away, stroking her skin as if wanting to linger. Goosebumps drifted over her as he stepped back. It was as if a tension in the stables had snapped, the release a kind of let-down, almost a disappointment.

'You may come and ride Kestia at any time you wish whilst you're here. Simply let the groom know.'

'What about you?'

The corner of his mouth turned upwards in a wry smile. 'I have a country to rule.'

'Is it enough?'

'It's all I have, and all I was born for. It must be enough.' He called over the groom, who led away his two charges. 'Now I'll leave you. We have the dinner tonight, where you'll accompany Stefano. I have much to do before then.'

He turned and strode out of the stables, as if hell itself were chasing him.

CHAPTER FIVE

ALESSIO STOOD BEFORE a mirror, carefully adjusting the white silk bow tie till it sat stiff and perfect at his throat. He wanted to rip it off, the infernal fabric too tight, the top buttons of his pristine shirt choking him. Instead he turned away, breathing slowly, slipping gold cufflinks adorned with the royal crest into the holes of his turned-back cuffs. Sealing them, and him, into place. He shrugged on his jacket, checked again that the Prince of Lasserno had been buttoned, cuffed and tied into his costume. Trying not to think of the afternoon. Of a woman with dark hair the colour of melted chocolate, flying over a fence on a horse. Her grief that twinned his own. The thrill of her warm skin under his fingers.

In Alessio's experience, women were cool, perfumed, and polished in all ways. Hannah had been none of those things today. Instead she'd been heat and fire and sweat and it was all he could do when the tears had gleamed in her eyes not to crush her to him and burn that grief away with a kiss. To see whether the skin of the rest of her was as soft as her cheek under his palm.

He flexed his fingers. Turned from the mirror and began to pace, his energy restless tonight, even after the ride. He'd held back on Apollo today in deference to what he'd believed was Hannah's lack of skill. That knowledge now pricked at him like an irritation. They'd wasted the afternoon on a sedate ride, when instead they could have challenged each other and their horses. Perhaps he'd go out again tomorrow, alone. But like every day, tomorrow his calendar was full. He supposed if he asked Stefano to find time his friend might suggest dropping the hospital visit, but that was the one thing he'd never cancel. Lasserno's sick children needed him, and he would not give up on them. Alessio dropped his head. Scrubbed his hands over his face. There was no time to rid himself of this sensation of needing to move. Not wanting to stop lest creeping thoughts caught up with him.

He checked his watch as a light tap sounded at the door. Almost time to leave.

'Enter.'

He expected Stefano but as the door cracked

open it was as if the breath had been punched from his chest. Hannah stood before him in a floor-length dress in the cool, silver-green of olive leaves, her hair up in some soft, loose style which fell about her face. Lips a perfect plum pout. Eyes a little smoky. She looked up at him and he couldn't breathe, his collar once again too tight, his bow tie choking him.

Alessio tugged at the neck of his shirt as her eyes widened. She was seated with Stefano at the dinner tonight, but, seeing her now, he wanted her with him in a way which defied rational thought. Better still, they could ignore the function and stay at the palace. Have a quiet candlelit dinner for two...

He shut down those errant thoughts. They had no place in his life.

'What are you doing here?' he asked, a little more harshly than he should have, but these were his private rooms. No woman had been in them before.

'Stefano told me to meet you here. Something about running late?'

That was unheard of. Stefano's views on punctuality were similar to his own. Alessio checked his phone and sure enough there was the message. He'd been so preoccupied he hadn't heard the alert.

Hannah stood, expectant. It wasn't quite time to leave and he couldn't have her waiting in the hall, so he stepped back, inviting her into the sitting room. Her long dress swished against the floor, sparkling at the hemline and part way up the skirt. Apart from that shine, the rest of her was unadorned. He couldn't shake the sense that she shouldn't go to the dinner without armour. Whilst the function was filled with more friends, such as they were, than enemies, even he knew how the worst of them could be. He could take care of himself. As he was Prince of Lasserno, people pandered to him. But any attack on Hannah he might not let go ignored. And he had to ignore her.

Except every fibre of his body rebelled at that knowledge.

'How were you after your ride?' Safer ground. He needed to make conversation rather than entertain thoughts of defending her like a prince from some fairy tale. Life was not a fantasy. Though she didn't appear to be faring much better, the way she looked at him in his suit. There was a prickling in his skin whilst she assessed him as if she were stripping him bare, breaking him down. Sometimes he wanted to know what she saw when she did that. What she was looking for when she cast her eyes over him. Did she find him lacking in any way?

Why the answer to those questions was imperative, he couldn't say.

'I'm a little stiff but that's no surprise, since I haven't ridden for almost nine years. But I had a long bath, which helped.'

Visions of her naked, lazing back in the large tub in her room, flushed with the heat of the water, assailed him and he couldn't get rid of them. What colour her nipples would be. Whether she'd be natural or waxed bare. And now those thoughts were planted in his head, they took root like weeds. This was insanity. Usually with women he had control. Around her his control frayed and shredded like rope being hacked by a knife.

'Excellent.' He could make light conversation. It was one of the things at which he excelled. 'You look…beautiful tonight.'

Not exactly where he wished to head, but he was being polite. Any man would say the same. Although it wasn't mere politeness driving him.

She looked like some sprite or will-o'-the-wisp, intent on leading him to his doom.

A soft flush of pink tinted her cheeks at the compliment. Who was there in her life to tell her she was beautiful? Was there anyone at all? The thought that no one might have said this to her recently seemed somehow wrong.

'Thank you.' Her voice was soft. Always that tone which was slightly lower and huskier than he expected, causing a tremor right through him, like fingernails scoring down his spine. And the change in her voice suggested that she was affected too. He grabbed on to that thought as if it were a golden nugget of hope.

He'd never had that hope or insecurity before. Women found him attractive. He had a wealth of experience to back up that certainty. But right now he didn't care about anyone else. He only cared that *this* woman was attracted to him, and Alessio didn't know why it mattered. Certainty was his friend. This sensation, of standing on shifting sands, was not.

She began to move, walking around the room as if inspecting it, her glorious dress glittering under the lights as she did.

'Would you like a seat?' he asked. It was as

if she were parading in front of him, and he couldn't take his thoughts from the way her bodice cinched at her slender waist. How her gauzy capped sleeves sat tantalisingly at her shoulders. Half on, half off, as if with the wrong shift they would fall and leave more of her glorious skin exposed, the cool, creamy sweep of her décolletage, which would no doubt haunt his dreams, naked and perfect. It should at least be adorned with some jewels, so they could distract him, rather than cause the near impossible-to-control desire to drop his gaze to the gentle swell of her cleavage.

'No. I'm a bit scared to sit down.' She brushed her hands across the fabric, which seemed to sit in multiple layers. When had the construction of a dress ever held such fascination for him? 'I don't usually wear things like this, and I don't want to crush it.'

His first thought was that she should wear dresses like this every night. The next thought was of him holding her in his arms, kissing her. Crushing her dress in the most satisfying of ways.

'You've no jewellery.'

Hannah cocked her head, as if what he'd said

was a kind of slight, when really he was only making conversation to stop the itch in his fingers, which tempted him to reach out and touch, to see how much softer she'd feel after her bath.

'No, *Your Highness.*' Those words contained no deference at all. She wielded them as a weapon. 'I didn't want to outshine you.'

A slight smile touched the corner of her lips. He should be offended, but he liked the way she didn't pander to him.

'I'm afraid you already have. No one will be paying any attention to me with such beauty in the room.'

The colour still ran high on her cheeks, but apart from that blush she seemed unaffected. 'Oh, dear. How does it feel, the risk that the spotlight won't be on you?'

A blessed relief. But it was something he could never admit, for the spotlight would never be turned away. 'I'm sure my fragile ego can handle the assault for one night, especially since I'm accompanied by you. Beauty has a way of outshining the beast.'

She snorted, the sound more cute from her than disdainful. 'You're more Prince Charming tonight than Beast.'

'Perhaps I was a beast this afternoon.'

Her gaze dropped to his mouth and held. Was she recalling his touch in the stables, wishing he'd kissed her? The burn of that recollection, the desire…it ignited and began to flare almost out of control. But he'd had years of practice managing it. No matter how much he might want her right now, it would pass. It always did.

'You obviously love your horses and had no idea of my experience. It was understandable. Anyway, it's well known that a *real* princess can tame the beast, and you'll have one of those soon. Isn't that the way the story goes?'

It should be. His longlist was now slimmed to a shortlist. But Alessio wasn't sure. He didn't care for the map of his life right now, the journey relentless most days, unwelcome on others. Required every day. He had no choices, the needs of his country forgotten too long by his father. His own desire to do better, to repair the damage done to his people, overcame any personal sentiments. But tonight, perhaps *just* for tonight, he could engage in a small moment of folly. Those glimpses of sadness Hannah had exposed this afternoon, the shadows which haunted her face from the loss she'd suffered, they hadn't quite left her. Fleeting happiness was what he could provide, and in his experience, women loved jewels. Though he wasn't sure about anything with Hannah. She didn't fit the familiar moulds. Still, he wanted to make *her* feel like a princess tonight.

'A woman should always outshine the man.'

'That's not the way it is in the animal kingdom.'

'I say that's the way it should be.'

'Are you pulling the prince card here? I'm the ruler…my rules?' Her eyes glittered with mirth under the lights. He wanted her covered in jewels that shone as much as she did, to keep that smile on her face.

'Wait here.'

He walked through his bedroom, to the dressing room. Behind a panel in the wall, he opened a safe. Drew out a rich purple velvet box. People wanted diamonds, rubies, emeralds, sapphires. The gaudy gems. In his hands was a necklace which matched Hannah's dress to perfection. Matched her, with its understated elegance. It might not have seemed as precious as the crown jewels, but to him it was more beautiful because of how uncommon it was. The stones were awash with the same grey-green as her dress, with swirls of gold like the bleeding colour from the watercolour pencils she'd shown him. The surrounding diamonds were an old mine cut, designed to show their true beauty in candlelight.

He tried not to think too hard about what he was doing as he closed the safe and returned to Hannah. These jewels he'd inherited. They were not part of the crown jewels his father had begun to plunder when needing a bauble to give away or for a bribe. These had been locked in the safe in his room too long. They needed to shine again.

Hannah stood with her back to him, gazing out of the window. Staring at the view into Lasserno's capital, glittering like her in the darkened landscape. As he entered the room she turned, those all-seeing eyes fixed on the box in his hands.

'What's that?'

'Adornments. They match your dress.'

Her eyes widened a fraction, her mouth opened. Shut.

'I'm getting the feeling this is a bit like a movie moment. I'm not sure I like it.'

'I promise you will, and you can always say no. But please look.' He opened the box and turned it to her. The jewels lay on pristine white satin inside.

'Oh.' She reached out and then drew back her fingers. 'What's the stone? The colours... And it looks like there are tiny ferns in it.'

'Dendritic agate. Most people don't appreciate its beauty. But the pattern is made in nature and it would have taken years to put together the complementing pieces. Far harder than matching other gemstones.'

'It looks old.' Her voice was a breathy whisper. The kind you wanted in your ear when making love. The whole of him tensed.

'About two hundred years or so. Everyone seeks out the sparkle of new gemstones, the brilliant cuts, but I prefer this. And the greens match your dress.'

'I can't. It's—'

'Try it on.' It seemed imperative now that she wear it. A drive he couldn't ignore. 'Come here.'

She edged to where he stood, near a gilt mirror. He took the cool, heavy necklace from its box. Reached over Hannah's head and draped it round her neck, settling the gems at her throat and securing the clasp. His breath disturbed fine hairs curling at her nape as they escaped her hairstyle. Goosebumps peppered her skin. He craved to run his hands over them. Feel the evidence of her pleasure under his fingertips.

Alessio looked up at her in the mirror, the moment so profoundly intimate and domestic it zapped through him like an electric shock. Instead of giving in to the desire threatening to overwhelm him, he stepped back.

'Do you like it?'

She reached her hand up, and tentatively touched the central stone. She smelled of the final days of autumn, like apples and the last of the season's roses. Rich and intoxicating.

'It's almost like an underwater scene.'

'It's perfect.'

'I can't wear this.' She shook her head. The diamonds twinkled as she moved. 'They're crown jewels.'

'They're not officially in the royal collection. They're mine to do with what I wish, and my wish is that you leave them on. Every woman should have the opportunity to wear something like this, at least once in her life. To feel like a princess.'

'That might have been Mum's nickname for me, but I'm no princess.'

Alessio wondered whether they had talked of Hannah marrying a prince, and whether her dream had died in the accident. He wasn't sure why it mattered, if it had.

'You look like one.'

It was as though the moment froze, with them standing so close in the room, as if time had paused and was giving them this small slice to cherish before wrenching them back into reality. But Alessio knew reality always intruded.

An alert chimed and here the world caught up with them like some spell had been broken. Then a knock sounded at the door.

'Enter.'

Stefano walked in, gave a brief bow.

'Your car has arrived.' He turned to Hannah. His gaze held at her neck for a heartbeat, that hesitation saying more than words could. Her hand fluttered to touch the necklace again, as if afraid someone would take it away. Stefano gave her a brief smile. 'Signorina Barrington.'

To Alessio, he raised an eyebrow.

'Do you know what you're doing?' The words were spoken in Italian, so Hannah couldn't understand.

Alessio checked the time on his watch. Straightened his bow tie. It was the first time in a *long* time that his friend had questioned him. From the moment he had received the call to say his mother was unwell, he'd known. His course unwelcome but set. Ignoring his needs and desires for the good of the country. He straightened his spine like the prince he was.

'*Ovviamente.*' Of course.

Stefano responded with nothing more than a curt nod as they left for the cars. And all the while on the journey to the dinner, Alessio's lie stuck like a fishbone in his throat.

They stood outside the doorway of a ballroom in a magnificent villa on the outskirts of the capital. Hannah had been told on the way here that this would be a more intimate function, but it didn't sound like it from the cacophony of voices drifting from the ballroom ahead. She touched the central stone of the magnificent necklace, sitting warm and heavy round her throat in a way that seemed comforting, the piece so beautiful she had almost wept when Alessio had shown it to her.

She'd loved the way he had looked at her tonight, after clasping the gems round her neck. As if she was someone precious. Special. Someone to be revered. The intensity of his gaze had left her tight and shivery, hot and cold all at once. It was how she felt about him, watching Alessio now in his black dinner suit, snowy white waistcoat and bow tie. Dressed so formally he looked…more. In control, in charge, masterful. For the tiniest of moments she allowed temptation to whisper that she'd love him to master her.

Hannah's cheeks heated with the illicit thought, but at least the lights were lower out here in the hall. She wouldn't look so much like a vividly toned root vegetable. No one paid her any attention anyway. Right now, Alessio and Stefano were in discussion with what appeared to be a master of ceremonies, who alternated between wringing his hands and bowing as if in apology as Stefano gesticulated.

Alessio stood back a little, his disapproval obvious in the way he held himself, his jaw hard as he checked his watch. Stiff, as if he were retreating into himself and rebuilding another persona by degrees. He glanced over at her, and she decided not to hang back as if this weren't her place. She'd been invited here. She had the dress, the heels, the jewels, and for one night she could be the princess in a story of her own making.

She walked over to the two men. 'Is there a problem?'

Alessio smiled, but the smile didn't touch his eyes. Fake. A mask and nothing more.

'There appears to have been an error. You've been seated next to me.'

She was supposed to sit with Stefano tonight, but a beat of something a lot like anticipation thrummed through her at the thought of being by Alessio's side. Still, she understood the impossibility of her desire and what was *not* being said. Alessio appearing with a woman would invite speculation which a deeply private man like him would despise.

Hannah pasted on her own fake smile. 'I'll change tables, then.'

'Changing tables means changing place cards and will invite more gossip.'

He turned and spoke in Italian to the worried-looking man still hovering in the doorway between the hall and where the dinner would be held. When Alessio finished, the man sagged a fraction and bowed a final time, before hurrying inside the ballroom.

'Come,' Alessio said to her. 'People know we're here. It's time to go in.'

'What did you say to him?'

'That wherever we're placed is suitable, but Stefano would miss your presence at his table.'

'Will he?'

There was something inscrutable about the way he looked at her.

'Any man would.'

The pleasure at those words slid through her with the potency of a shot of spirits. A sensation all too intoxicating to be good for her, so she tried to ignore it. Hannah moved into position and Stefano took her arm, given he'd walk her inside, but Alessio in front held all her attention. He was entirely changed, the metamorphosis into Lasserno's ruler complete. Strength and stability radiated from him like a beacon. Solid. Uncompromising. And yet behind the mask of his public persona, she still glimpsed the true man simmering underneath. He carried himself with an unnatural stiffness, and a tightness around the eyes suggested he wasn't entirely happy in this new skin.

The master of ceremonies announced something to the assembled guests she couldn't understand. The noise of chairs scraping back interrupted the murmurs from the room. A hush descended as everyone waited. Alessio's shoulders rose then fell as if he took a deep breath, then with a straightening of his spine he stepped forward through the doorway as she and Stefano followed. Her eyes adjusted to the brighter lights of the room and she gasped at the sparkling chandeliers, towering floral decorations and gleaming silver candelabras adorning the opulent ballroom. About fifty people stood round tables scattered through the space and every face was turned to Alessio as he waited at the top of the stairs, allowing the assembled guests to take their fill of him, their Crown Prince, and his most honoured guest. It was a dizzying sensation to realise there were a hundred eyes on them as he made his way down the sweeping marble staircase into the room, a leader of his nation in all ways. Arresting and intoxicating.

As they walked through the room Hannah touched her necklace again, almost as a reflex. The curdle of something like fear slithered in her belly but the jewels reminded her that she had a place here tonight. They moved through tables to their seat and people stared and whispered as she passed. When they reached their table, Stefano pulled out her chair.

'I'll see you later, Hannah,' he murmured. It was said quietly enough to seem private, loud enough to pique people's interest. The game of deflection had begun. She merely smiled. Ignored everyone's curious stares as she sat and accepted a glass of champagne from the waiter, thanking the man who poured it for her.

'Ladies, gentlemen.' The table descended into silence as Alessio spoke. 'I'm pleased to introduce Signorina Hannah Barrington. My portrait artist, who has taken two weeks from her hectic schedule to be here before returning to England.'

It was a statement of intent. One she understood, but something about it left her feeling deflated, like a leftover balloon from a long-forgotten party. Alessio named the people at the table for her benefit. Counts, countesses, the Prime Minister and his wife. Lasserno's aristocracy. The country's *Who's Who.*

A few people nodded with interest or stared as if in disbelief at the position she held, sitting to Alessio's left. She could understand why. He was a man in his prime. Available, a prince. Who wouldn't want to be her? They must know he was looking for a bride. Did they assume she was in the running? Her throat tightened and she took a sip of her champagne, the bright bubbles sparkling on her tongue and slipping too easily down her throat. Surely everyone here knew he was looking for a princess? And yet as she watched the other guests' open looks of avarice, she realised this dinner held all the danger of picking her way through a room filled with broken glass in bare feet.

She steeled her spine. Whatever these people might think, they were all wrong and she'd show them. Alessio had to deal with this every day and Hannah couldn't imagine how wearing it must be. She glanced at him now, making easy conversation with the Prime Minister.

'How do you find His Highness's hospitality?' asked a man in a uniform festooned with medals. She didn't like the supercilious way his brow rose when he spoke to her.

Still, her place at this table wasn't to make trouble but to smooth it over. Hannah smiled. 'His Highness is a gracious host, as one would expect.'

'Are you spending much time in his presence?'

The corner of the man's mouth turned up in a smirk. 'For research purposes, of course.'

People near them began to watch the exchange, whilst Alessio seemed engrossed in his own conversation. Around the table the air vibrated with tension, a warning. This question was a kind of trap, but she wouldn't fall into it, because no matter how strong and uncompromising he seemed, Hannah realised that Alessio needed shielding. All these people were vultures waiting for others to hunt down their prey and then pick over the carcass left.

She refused to be their victim.

'He's managed to fit me into his hectic schedule.'

The man's smile in response appeared knowing, when he really had no clue. 'I'm *sure* he has.'

Those words carried a weight and meaning everyone sitting at the table would understand. She pretended to be oblivious. To rise above it, since innocence was her weapon.

'Enough to sketch and make the studies I need for the coronation portrait.'

'You're young to receive such an illustrious commission,' said a countess wearing a shimmering gold dress of liquid satin and diamonds round her neck the size of pigeon eggs. 'You must have quite prodigious...talents.'

Hannah swallowed. She couldn't stop the fire igniting in her belly at these insinuations. She knew her worth, the work and the sacrifice she put into her art. Her achievements. She didn't care what the guests here thought of her. Alessio was the one getting the portrait. She'd never paint any of these people, no matter how much they offered. Even if they *begged*, because she didn't want to know them.

Not the way she was coming to know Alessio.

'I'll leave that judgement to others. My job's to paint. To find the essence of a person.'

'And have you found the essence of His Highness?' Those words were delivered with a venomous smile. One which appeared friendly but carried a sting.

'Not yet. But I've never painted a prince before.'

A few people murmured at her response, but she couldn't understand what was being said. They seemed friendly enough, so she suspected it wasn't a criticism. She hardly cared. They could think what they wanted. She knew the truth. Then next to her, Alessio straightened.

She could almost feel the electric crackle of him from his seat.

'I suggest, Contessa, that you do your research. Signorina Barrington has won some of the most prestigious portrait competitions in the world. She is the best. There is *no one* more qualified to paint my coronation portrait than her.'

His voice bristled with warning, sharp and cold. Now everyone at the table stared at them. Whilst his chill was meant to give a clear message, to her his voice was like being immersed in a warm bath. She basked in his defence, even though it would likely cost him. For a man whose private life was deliberately opaque, he'd allowed the door to crack open a chink, showing in the tiniest of ways that she mattered.

She couldn't thank him in public, so she smiled benevolently as if praise like this were given to her every day. But, since they sat next to each other, she moved her thigh towards his until their knees touched. A tiny gesture to say thank you in a way she couldn't immediately vocalise. Hannah applied the smallest amount of pressure, to let Alessio know her move wasn't accidental. The fingers of his left hand flexed on the tablecloth and he pressed back. The thrill of that secret acknowledgement bubbled through her like the sparkle of champagne. They sat knee to knee, calf to calf, ankle to ankle, and even through the layers of her dress it was as if she could sense the heat burning between them.

The conversation changed after his intervention, the flow of it around the table broken by the royal toast. Hannah stood with everyone else and the sense of loss she suffered at the lack of that supportive touch seemed almost visceral, as if something magical had been broken. She watched Alessio, who managed to look utterly alone even when surrounded by this host of people. There was a blankness about him which showed that any emotion had been well and truly shuttered and locked down. She didn't know how he managed to eat, other than out of politeness. She sampled the beautiful-looking food and, whilst delicious, it held no appeal. This crowd would likely poison your meal as anything else. It was almost a surprise that Alessio didn't have an official food taster, they were all so toxic.

'Have you ridden with His Highness?' the Countess asked, after they'd resumed their seats. She was surprised the woman hadn't accepted Alessio's put-down, but she was young enough to be interested in him for herself and there was a determined gleam in her eye. 'He's known as a passionate horseman.'

She decided to tell the truth because enough people had seen her ride with Alessio to make a lie far worse.

'Yes. Have you?'

Even though she wasn't looking at him, she was aware as Alessio stiffened, so attuned to him now that she could sense the slow freeze again. He shifted as she pressed her leg to his once more. Letting him know she had this. That he'd protected her, but it was okay for him to accept her help too.

The Countess's mouth thinned. If looks were daggers, Hannah would be properly skewered. 'No, I have never been invited to ride by His Highness, but it would be my *extreme* pleasure to do so.'

Hannah raised an eyebrow in a way she hoped looked imperious. 'Perhaps one day, if you're a good enough rider, you'll be lucky and get your chance.'

She didn't think the woman had the care, intuition or skill to be allowed anywhere near Alessio's beloved horses. Hannah only realised now the privilege she'd been afforded being allowed to ride Kestia whenever she wished.

The Countess turned her attention to Alessio. 'Your Highness, it's an uncommon honour you invited Signorina Barrington to sit at your table.'

He fixed the woman with a cold glare. 'It's you who should be honoured, to have such a prestigious artist in your company.'

'The sad truth,' Hannah said, no doubt breaking protocol with her interruption but not caring less, 'is there was a terrible mix-up in the beginning. I was meant to sit with Stefano.'

She was coming to realise gossip was the currency of value fuelling these people, so she'd give them something to talk about. She glanced over to where Stefano sat at a distant table and gave a little wave. He raised his champagne flute and toasted her in response.

'You were looking forward to sitting with His Highness's private secretary?'

'Oh, yes. Very much,' Hannah said. 'But there's always tomorrow.'

This could have been a pleasant evening in a magnificent room, with exquisite food and wine. Her fantasy for just one night. She resented the people here intent on ruining it. Some of them were trying to goad Alessio's responses, to play a game in which there could be no winners.

The thing was, they hadn't counted on her.

Alessio adjusted the napkin on his lap. As he did so his hand brushed hers, feather-light. So fleeting it could have been a mistake, but she knew it hadn't been. Her breathing hitched, a shiver of pleasure running through her, settling low and heavy.

Tonight, she and Alessio were a team. None of the people here could touch them. She ate some more food, sipped more champagne. All the time exquisitely aware of the man sitting next to her. And as their legs touched under the table once more, their secret, she prayed this dinner was over soon and that she'd done enough.

CHAPTER SIX

THE JOURNEY BACK to the palace had been in near silence. There was too much going through Alessio's head for him to say anything at all. The sly comments, the innuendos, all directed at one woman.

A woman who'd seen fit to defend him in the face of obvious attacks.

'Do you need to discuss this evening's events?' Stefano asked as they walked towards the royal suite. Hannah remained silent. Alessio wanted to know how she felt, given everything that had passed. 'And would you like me to take Signorina Barrington on a very public sightseeing tour tomorrow? A quiet word in the right news organisation's ear and—'

'No, and no press.'

'If we used them properly, it could be to your advantage. They fabricate news about you, since they get none. Why not feed the beast a different story?'

This old argument between them could wait for another day. He didn't want Hannah used to deflect attention from his own errors. Inviting her into the hornet's nest was his mistake. She'd done enough tonight by tolerating the dinner. For that alone he must thank her.

'I need to place the necklace in the safe,' he said. Hannah stood there with her head held high, looking more like royalty than he felt after tonight's efforts. Lasserno's aristocracy had not crowned themselves in glory.

Hannah reached behind her neck to undo the clasp and he shook his head.

'You can remove it in my room,' he said, then added to Stefano, 'We can speak tomorrow if there's a need.'

Stefano gave Hannah a lingering look, nodded, then left.

Alessio opened the door of his suite and walked inside with Hannah following. The burn in his gut overtook him now, raging close to the surface over the way she'd been treated. All the while his emotions mingled with something softer, more tempting. She'd defended him, worked to ensure there were no rumours about them. Pretended *for* him. That protectiveness was unfamiliar in his experience. Its allure potent. The memory of their knees pressing together, the hidden support…he couldn't put it out of his mind. In his role as Prince of Lasserno he was tasked as protector of a nation. The weight of all decisions fell on his shoulders. Tonight, Hannah had relieved some of his burden and he could never thank her enough.

'Would you like a drink?' He rarely resorted to alcohol, avoiding any kind of excess, but he needed something to dull the immediacy of his anger.

She shook her head. Standing under the soft lights, glittering and perfect. As if this were her place. But it couldn't be, no matter the temptation.

'No, I think I've had more than enough wine. But feel free.'

He smiled at the audacity of her giving him permission in his own rooms. She was a constant challenge to his position, and he feared he was enjoying the challenge far too much.

'I will.' He poured a slug of amber fluid into a glass.

'You are the Prince and all. You can do what you like.'

The weight of responsibility sometimes threatened to crush him, and yet he couldn't yield to it. He took a swig of his drink, the burn of the spirit doing nothing to ease the emotions sliding through his veins. Anger, desire. A dangerous mix when coupled with a beautiful, uncompromising woman.

A woman who seemed to be shifting from foot to foot, as if she were in discomfort.

'Are you all right?'

She winced. 'Do you mind if I take off these heels? They're like a torture device.'

'Feel free.' He lifted his glass to take another swig of Scotch but stopped as Hannah grabbed on to the corner of a chair, kicked off the heels and wiggled her toes in the carpet, closing her eyes and sighing as she did so. 'Heaven.'

Alessio couldn't tear his gaze from her toes, peeking out from under the hem of her dress. Red. He swallowed. Bright. Vibrant. Red. For some reason that bold colour was unlike one he thought she might wear. It surprised him. As if he were being allowed to glimpse some secret about her. He didn't know why a need pounded through him now, his heart like an anvil being struck by the blacksmith's hammer. They were only feet. But that intimacy again almost undid him.

'I'm sorry,' Alessio said.

She shrugged. 'For formal occasions I know they're expected. Beauty is pain and all that. I just don't have any need to wear heels around the farm.'

'Not about the shoes.' Alessio couldn't look at her right now. Instead he turned to the mirror and tugged his bow tie undone. Wrenched the top button of his shirt open, crushing the perfectly pressed cotton under his fingers. Even then his clothes choked him. 'The people.'

She came into view, reflected behind him. Picked up a small porcelain figurine of a horse that decorated a side table, inspecting it, running her fingers over the smooth surface. What he wouldn't give right now to have those fingers running over his skin instead. He took another sip of his drink. No good would come of those thoughts. His responsibility was to look after her as an employee, not dream of Hannah undressing him with her gentle, stroking fingers.

Yet it was this last thought he couldn't get out of his head.

'I'm used to the mean girls,' she said. 'You meet a few.'

Alessio wheeled around. She was precious. She shouldn't have to deal with anyone cruel. 'Where would you meet people like *that*? Your clients?'

'No, my clients are nice…' she skewered him with her insightful gaze and smiled sweetly '…in the main. I came across them at boarding school after my parents died. Girls could be cruel to an orphan like me.'

'Oh, *bella*.' Her eyes widened a fraction as the term of endearment slipped out unchecked. He started forward, wanting to comfort her, but that wasn't his role. It never could be. Though the reasons for that seemed to be getting a little hazy. 'Why were you at a boarding school?'

She walked to a portrait on the wall, another glowering ancestor, all a reminder of the job he had to do for Lasserno. He ensured they stared down on him from every private wall in the palace so he would never falter.

'My aunt and uncle were my guardians. They didn't have children of their own and said it would give me stability.'

'Did it?'

'No. It was awful. I didn't…cope. So they

brought me home and sent me to the local school. Not prestigious, but small and familiar.'

He could barely imagine the pain she had suffered, both parents lost. Being sent away from everything she'd known. The unfairness tore at him. At least when his mother had died he'd had some sympathetic courtiers, given his father was of no use.

'I enjoyed boarding school. Away from the constraints of the palace. Away from my parents' cold war.' The open battles over his father's infidelity. 'It seemed like bliss in comparison, even though boys can be brutal.'

There was a softness in the way she looked at him now, like sympathy, when he was owed none from her. 'Being a prince, you would have been top of the tree.'

He threw back the last of his drink. Tempting to have more, but not sensible in the circumstances. 'That's not always the best position to be in. It brings with it a certain entitlement which I needed to unlearn.'

She had an uncanny way of getting him to speak the truth of everything. He put his glass down on a side table. The *domesticity* of this scene assailed him once more. As if she should be here. As if this was her rightful place. A delectable sense of inevitability slid through him.

As if there was no other place she should *ever* be.

'You learned that at least. If you had one wish, what would it be?'

Her questions. Funny how she'd stopped asking the ones on her infernal list. However, this one seemed appropriate. He had so many wishes. That he had a sibling, so he was not all alone. That his parents had had a happy marriage like some of those he'd witnessed with his school friends. That his mother had not died. But there was one wish, above all. It came to the fore on nights like tonight, when he realised every choice was taken away by duty. *That* wish pricked at him like a dagger between the ribs, sliding true to his heart. His deepest secret, and some days his greatest shame.

'Not being the Prince of Lasserno.' Being an ordinary man with ordinary choices. He looked over at the decanter of Scotch sitting on the sideboard. He'd never drowned his regrets in alcohol before, but tonight he wanted to down the whole bottle. 'And you?'

Hannah paled, her skin translucent in the

lights. The antique diamonds glittering at her throat. She should always be in diamonds, this woman. Draped in jewels to frame her beauty. Her head dropped. She scuffed at the carpet with her pretty painted toes.

'I wish I'd been in the car with my parents.' Her voice was so soft he almost didn't hear it, but the force of what she said struck him like a blow. His whole body rebelled at the thought she might not be here, that if she'd been in that car the world would be without her brilliance.

'No!' He cut through the air with his hand as her eyes widened. He was surprised by his own vehemence. The visceral horror that this was how she might feel. 'You do *not* wish that.'

He strode towards her, the hectic glitter in her eyes telling him tears were close. He wasn't good with tears. His mother had spilled enough of them in his presence, railing against his father. He'd been inured to most of them in the end, learning to comfort without feeling the pain himself.

The threat of Hannah's ripped at the fabric of his being.

'It's my wish. It can be what I want.'

'Survivor's guilt.' As if those two words could

ease her dark thoughts. Had she had counselling after her parents had passed? Her aunt and uncle had sent her away to boarding school. Perhaps they'd expected her to get over things without the help a teenager might need after such a loss. 'If this is the way you feel then you should—'

'You don't understand.' She turned away from him, wrapped her arms round her waist. 'If I hadn't travelled with my friend that afternoon, we'd have gone a different way home. We wouldn't have been on that road. The tractor wouldn't have been on the bend. They might...'

They might be alive.

Alessio went to her, placed his hands gently on her shoulders. Her skin was warm, soft as satin. He circled his thumbs on her exposed flesh. She leaned back into him. As if taking, for a moment, the meagre solace he could provide.

'We both want things we can't have,' he murmured.

'You could give up the throne. I can't turn back time.'

He let out a long, slow breath. Occasionally in his fantasies he'd allow himself to simply be a man, but he had the luxury of being able to think that way. 'No. I can't. I have a duty to my people and that duty is more important than anything. More important than a man's desires.'

She disengaged from him and he mourned the loss of his hands on her skin, the warmth of her. 'At least you can change things.'

'I'll always be the leader of Lasserno.'

'Not everything has to be for duty. You talk about finding the perfect princess. Is that duty as well?'

'All that I do is for my country.'

'Then what feeds the man's soul?'

He walked to the windows of the palace overlooking his capital. The city, glittering in the late evening like a bright jewel. One entirely in his care. 'The man doesn't exist in isolation from the Prince. They're one and the same.'

'What about love?'

'What about it?'

'You could marry for that. Love's not about duty.'

Alessio wheeled around. He knew this story, an age-old one. Love had no place in his life. He'd seen how it ate away, destroyed when one party stopped loving the other, or perhaps had never loved them in the first place. His parents' relationship had been the best evidence of that.

It inured him to ever seeking anything more for himself. If duty it was to be, then that would extend to his princess, who'd understand the constraints of royalty, the expectations of her role.

Sure he'd had promises before…of love, of adoration…all so a woman could get a crown on her head too. He could never be sure of anyone, whether they wanted the man, the money or his family's name, especially after Allegra's efforts. Better he found someone who knew what this was, a dynastic endeavour. Protecting his country from a vacuum, nothing more. In many ways Hannah was the same as others, accepting the exorbitant fee he'd offered her to paint his portrait. The suspicion overran him, needy and unfamiliar. Had he not been the Prince of Lasserno, would she have agreed to paint him with no complaints? Probably. And that was something he should never forget. Even though tonight, she had seen fit to protect him at her own expense.

'And who would I find to love? You?'

Hannah's eyes widened, and then she laughed in a mocking kind of way, as if what he'd said was ridiculous. 'Me? That's absurd.'

Which was not the answer he'd been expecting. He'd expected a shy glance, some fluttering of eyelids. A woman playing coy at the hint something more might be on offer. Any reaction other than suggestions of foolishness on his part.

'Many women want to be a princess.'

'When they're little girls, perhaps. But I'm all grown up, and those kinds of dreams die when you realise that's all they are. Silly, glitter-covered fantasies which tarnish as soon as you expose them to reality. I'm an artist. A commoner. We don't marry princes.'

Had her dreams died with her parents? He wanted to rail against it. She should be allowed to have the fantasy she could be whatever she wanted. He couldn't have that dream, but that didn't mean the same was unavailable to her.

'What feeds the woman's soul?'

The flush ran over her cheeks. 'My art consumes me. When I paint, nothing else exists. It's all I've wanted for a long time. It's enough.'

It sounded like an excuse.

'You look like a princess. And tonight, at the table, you acted like a queen. No royalty I know would have done better.'

It was as if she'd protected one of her own, when no one apart from Stefano ever leapt to his defence, only tried to tear him down. The warm kernel of something lit in his chest. Bright, perfect. Overlaid with an intoxicating drumbeat down low. Desire that was dark, tempting and forbidden. Something to be taken care of by himself, on the rare occasion it afflicted him, or with a willing partner who knew what this was. A few hours of passion, nothing more.

Not with a woman he'd begun to crave with a kind of obsession. *Never* that.

A slow stain of colour crept up her throat. A gentle smile on her lips. The obvious pleasure in a compliment letting him know she was still a woman underneath all her talk otherwise.

'Thank you. I'll let you in on a secret. For a little while, I felt like one. The make-up, a pretty dress. Some exquisite jewellery that isn't mine. It's all smoke and mirrors really. But for one night, I'll admit it was fun.'

She didn't understand. It wasn't the trappings that had her competing with royalty, but her demeanour. The way she had stood up to those who tried to cut her down. The way she had stood up for him…

'What if for one night, it's what we could have?' The urgency of his need gripped him. The fantasy that he could have her for this moment.

Every part of him began to prickle with anticipation, the hum of pleasure coursing through his blood. 'If we could pretend that I'm simply a man, and you're simply a woman.'

'That you're not the Prince of Lasserno? Are you asking me to grant your wish?'

A pulse beat at the base of her throat, an excited kind of fluttering that told him she wanted this too.

'And I'd treat you like the princess that you are.'

Her pupils expanded, drowning the rockpool green of her eyes till the colour was a mere sliver. Her lips parted, as if the oxygen had been sucked from the room, and he sensed it too. The tightening of his chest as if he couldn't fill his lungs.

She stood in front of him, glowing, beautiful in a way which evoked physical pain. He wanted her so badly he would drop to his knees and beg her like some supplicant so long as she granted him one evening, for both of them to lose themselves in the pretence they could be something other than who they were.

'Bella?' Her blood-red toes curled into the carpet. He clenched his hands to fists so he wouldn't reach out, touch. Take. 'I will do nothing unless

you say yes. The choice, it is yours alone. Stay, or go.'

He had the power here. An imbalance she must never feel beholden to. He needed her to crave him as much as he craved her, to a kind of distraction.

She licked her lips. The mere peek of her tongue almost undid him. How he wanted to plunder that mouth. Tear the clothes from her body. Rip apart the fabric of both their lives for a night of pleasure, lost in her arms.

'If I'm a princess tonight, then who are you?'

The fantasy wove around him. Something which allowed them to forget who they were and what they were doing here.

'I'm the frog you're about to kiss.'

'But that means you'll turn into a prince.'

'I won't be Prince of Lasserno. I'll be *your* prince.'

Hers alone.

Hannah's lips curled into a wicked smile. 'For only one night.'

It wasn't a question, and in a strange way that gave him some comfort. But the thought laced him with a kind of pain, that when the sun rose in the morning this blissful, illicit fantasy would be over.

'That's all it can ever be. Sex has a way of changing things, but it can't change this,' he said, as much of a warning to him as it was to her. Though the fantasy wove into a reality, where she could turn him into someone else for a few hours, because they both willed it.

'And what about duty?'

'Tonight?' It could only be one night and nothing else. That was all he would allow himself. And for him, that would be enough. 'Duty can go to hell.'

Duty can go to hell.

The words rang through her like some clarion call. He stood there, jaw hard. Hands clenched to fists at his sides. His bow tie hanging loose, and the top of his shirt unbuttoned to show the dark hair at his throat. Yet he wouldn't come to her. She knew it. She saw it in the tense set of his body. He wanted her to decide. And she craved him, with a zeal that made little sense to her. She'd never been particularly interested in sex, or so she had always thought, the idea of getting too close to someone, letting anyone in, crushing the breath right out of her. Caring was dangerous. Loving, even more so. But around Alessio, there was no common sense. As if he were all the oxygen in the room, as if to breathe she had to have him.

She wanted to walk into his arms, into all that strength. Bury her nose to the hollow at the base of his throat. Let every part of him overwhelm her. She took a step. The first. It wasn't so hard because this was a moment of fantasy where they could pretend to be other people. Alessio flexed his fingers as she took another step, and another. And only when she stood so close that his warmth seeped into her, did he wrap his arms round her, as strong as she'd imagined them to be. He dropped his head as if in slow motion. She rose on her toes and their lips touched. The warm press of skin to skin. Gentle, strangely innocent in a way that almost broke her heart. She dropped back, looked into his all-dark eyes, the pupils drowning out the velvet brown.

'Look,' she whispered, her voice cracking. A hesitation between them as if everything was tentative and the universe waited. 'I've made a prince.'

And then it was as if the world exploded around

them. Alessio groaned and took her face in his hands, crushing his lips to hers. She met him, her hands on his chest, fingers curling into the strong muscles there. She had no experience, but this seemed to lack all finesse, drawn from pure need. Their tongues touched, battled, as if each were trying to win over the other. Her body was all heat and fire, her exquisite dress of fine fabric a scraping interruption to his fingers on her overheated skin. She slipped her hands under his jacket, over the shoulders, tugging because every piece of clothing between them was a travesty. He let her face go, tore the jacket from his body. Tossed it to the floor.

'Your dress. I don't trust myself.'

She barely did her *own* self. But she reached round with trembling fingers and slid the zip down, slowly. As if this were a kind of performance, because she was transfixed by the hooded rapture in his eyes as he watched. There was no time for nerves, no time for doubts. Not here, not now. Tonight she *was* a princess, and she could do and have anything she wanted.

And how she wanted Alessio.

The dress slumped from her shoulders as she shrugged out of the bodice. The fabric slid over her body, fell to the floor. She stepped out of it, as if it were a sea of foam on the ground and she was leaving the ocean, reborn, in only the exquisite lace bra and panties which she'd purchased to match the dress. The single extravagance she'd allowed when preparing her trip to Lasserno. Her skin seemed too tight, as if she were a butterfly ready to burst from the chrysalis. It was as if for the past nine years she'd been in stasis, waiting. And now she'd been changed on a cellular level.

Hannah began to walk forward towards Alessio and he held up a hand.

'Wait. I want to look at you. To always remember your beauty.'

There were so many things that would be left unsaid tonight, but how precious these moments were would not be one of them. Now wasn't the time to be shy, but to be brave.

'I need to see you too,' she whispered, unsure as to whether her voice was loud enough with all the emotion trembling through it. Alessio's throat convulsed with a swallow which told her all she needed to know, that he'd heard her plea. He grabbed his bow tie, dragged it from round his neck and dropped it on the floor. Undid a button on his shirt, then another and another. Tugged the zinc-white fabric from the waist of his trousers, tossing it aside the way of his coat and bow tie. She inhaled sharply at the sight before her, his broad shoulders, the muscles of his arms all sculpted and bronzed. The hair at his chest, dusting the muscles there, trailing down, darkening and disappearing at his trouser waistband. Her fingers became restless to run them through the crisp hair. To touch. He undid his belt, drew it slowly from his trousers before tossing it aside. Her eyes dropped as he gripped the top of his trousers. Even though they were black, the evidence of his arousal was bold and obvious.

She'd done that to him.

'Like what you see?'

'I'd like to see more.'

He chuckled and the ripple of it rolled through her, like a promise for something she didn't know she'd been waiting for. Anticipation at its finest.

'Your wish is my command, *Principessa*.'

A thrill shivered through her, that she had any sway over this man. That he stood there, tense with his physical masculine beauty, waiting for her next word.

'Slowly.'

The corner of his mouth kicked up and he did exactly as she demanded. It was as if each notch on the zip took an age. Almost as if time were standing still. The leisurely, deliberate tease all for her as he hooked his hands into the waistband of his trousers and his underwear. The heat of this moment flamed in her cheeks. The boldness of it, all because of what she desired. It could careen out of control at any second, but for now this was hers. Alessio bent at the waist as his trousers passed his thighs, everything hidden, then they slipped to the floor and he rose. Stepped out of the superfine black wool and kicked them and his underwear away.

He stood straight, allowing her eyes to take their fill. She might be inexperienced, but she'd seen naked men before. In art, on the internet, in life-drawing classes. This, however, was more than she had ever experienced. A perfect man, drawn by the hand of angels. Too real to be human, yet undoubtedly flesh and blood. His arousal, because of her, intoxicating.

'I need to touch you. For you to touch me.' His voice was tight, as if he were in pain, and she understood. The ache inside her built and built. She felt she might double over with need, self-combust if their hands were not on one another soon.

'Yes. *Please.*'

He made it to her in a few strides, hands hot and hard on her hips, slipping round to her buttocks, pulling her close and against him. Burying his face in her neck and breathing her in. His lips kissing and skimming the sensitive skin there till she moaned. He slid his hands up her back as she shivered and quaked under his exquisite touch. Unhooked her bra. Slipped it over her arms and let it fall to the floor. He moved his hands to cup her breasts, stood back a mere fraction to look, brushed his thumbs to her nipples and they tightened with a burning pleasure. He looked down at her with reverence, as if she were a kind of revelation.

'Touch me,' he groaned and released one breast, taking her hand in his. Guiding it between them. Clasping it tight around his hard length. He hissed in a breath as he thrust into her palm, dropping his head back, and the tendons on his neck stood out, tense and as if he were in agony. She marvelled at the feel of him, silk over steel, and at his size, which she knew on a biological level should fit her, yet on a pure female level an uncertain niggle like fear began to seed and grow.

Fear had no place here, not tonight on her one evening allowing herself to be the princess in this fantasy. A night to give, take, indulge, before going back to real life, or her new version of it.

His grip on her hand loosened. He left her to stroke him up and down in the rhythm he'd set, returning his attention to her nipples, which were tight and aching. She shifted under his ministrations, *needing* him. It would be easy to ignore the obvious, not tell him about her inexperience, but this would do a disservice to them both, and she'd allow *nothing* to interfere with tonight.

She let him go and he opened his eyes, his lips apart. Eyes glazed and unfocused with pleasure.

'Alessio, I...' She hesitated when this was not the time for it. Now was the time to be bold. To take what she wanted for herself. He stopped teasing her nipples, rested his hands gently on her hips. Looked down at her with the slightest of frowns, of concern, she thought, and the warmth of realisation flooded her. She traced her hands up his body, to rest on the firm swell of his pectoral muscles, as the dark hair on his chest pricked and teased under her fingertips.

'You have something to say, *bella*?'

'I—I've never done this before.'

His grip on her hips tightened and released. 'This?'

'Sex. Any of it.'

His eyes widened a fraction. Then he wrapped his strong arms round her and drew her close into his embrace. The tears pricked at her eyes. Her virginity wasn't something she'd ever thought much of. It simply *was*. A fact. A reality. She'd never believed it merited much thought, until now.

'I'm your first.' The words were muffled and hot, murmured into her hair.

In everything.

'Yes.'

He stroked a hand up and down her spine. Light, tender brushes, and goosebumps sprinkled over her skin, as soft and warm as a spring shower.

'A better man would send you to bed on your own.'

'A better man wouldn't leave me feeling like this.' She pulled back and his arms fell loose. Hannah looked up at him. His pupils were drowning out the colour of his eyes till they were almost black. He was still hard and hot against her belly.

'Like what?' he ground out, all gravel and darkness.

'Empty. Like I'm going to die if you're not inside me. I *hurt* for wanting you so badly.'

His nostrils flared, lips parted a fraction. 'I won't leave you. I'll make it good for you. I promise.'

He slipped his hand to her left nipple again. Toying with it. Harder now. A light pinch.

'Do you like that?' he murmured.

She arched her back into him with the bright spark of pleasure rushing straight between her legs. Not so gentle then, and the slow burn between them became hotter and hotter.

'*Yes.*' Her voice was a sigh, nothing more.

'I can take the pain away,' he said as he eased her panties from her body till they slipped down her legs. 'You'll be screaming tonight from pleasure.'

Alessio slipped his hand between their bodies, between her thighs. Gentle strokes where she needed him most. It was too much and not enough all at the same time. She moved against him, desperate for more. Desperate to be filled, to be overwhelmed by him. She couldn't look at him now. Closed her eyes as if to hold on to the sensation so it would never end.

Then he slowed. Slid a finger inside her. Her fingers clawed into the hard muscles of his chest as he stroked something deep in her body, making Hannah quiver and quake with a flood of heat between her legs. 'I'll take care of you,' he murmured gently into her ear, kissing feather-light where his breath had stroked at her skin.

She clung round his neck because she'd fall if she didn't. Riding his hand like a woman who was a stranger to her.

Her head tipped back, and his lips were on hers. Soft, passionate. She opened and let him in. Their tongues touched, tangled together. She craved for him to invade every part of her. His fingers brushing her nipple, the sense of him deep inside, thrusting with one finger, then another.

'Let go, *bella*.' He whispered the words against her lips before crushing them to his again, adding a thumb to brush over her clitoris in soft, insistent strokes. He was everywhere, her world. She was burning like the hottest flame, till she was sure her skin would blister with it.

Then she came, cracked in two as if Alessio had torn her apart with pleasure. Screaming as he'd promised, in a rush of perfect, blinding heat.

Alessio breathed in the scent of her, the brightness of her perfume, the dark musk of her arousal, as she clenched hot and wet round his fingers. Then the weight of her arms round his neck intensified, as if her knees were giving out underneath her. He swept Hannah into his arms, her body soft and limp, her eyes glazed with arousal, a flush of colour tinting her cheeks, her chest. So beautiful in that dying blush of pleasure it almost caused him physical pain. He dropped his mouth to hers, her lips soft and yielding like the rest of her. All slick and hot and wet.

The privilege of being granted her trust flared inside him. He silently vowed it would be good for her, *better* than good. He wanted these hours with her to transcend mere sex. Something to be remembered, treasured, especially given it was her first time.

There would be no disappointing Hannah tonight. On the contrary, he feared she would be a revelation to shake the foundations of his being. He laid her gently on the covers of his bed, his body trembling with the desire to be inside her, where his fingers had been. But he would make sure tonight was about her. Her pleasure first and foremost.

Her eyes lay closed, the beautiful lashes feathering on her cheeks. He allowed her the bliss of the comedown from her orgasm. Perhaps her first at the hands of another. Marvelled at her body, splayed with abandon on the bed before him. Settled himself between her thighs where he could smell the sweet scent of arousal, the necklace at her throat like a jewelled symbol of his possession, making this all the more erotic. He dropped his head and licked, the taste of her like a drug shooting straight into his veins, and she groaned as he toyed with her. Worshipping her in the best way he knew how.

Her back arched from the bed as she gripped and released the covers.

'Alessio… I…it's too much.'

He ceased his ministrations. Stroked his thumbs gently on the insides of her thighs. As much as she said it was too much, her back arched, bringing her body closer to his mouth.

'Relax. You have no idea how much your body can take but I can show you. I can show you it all. Let me pleasure you,' he murmured against her, so close to where he wanted his mouth to be it almost watered.

'Yes.' The word came like the softest of exhales, the sweetest capitulation, and he began his gentle ministrations again, the light flicking of his tongue, till she thrashed on the bed, her words indecipherable. She thrust her hand into his hair and gripped tight, the bright needles of pain causing the heat of passion to roar through him like lava in his blood. He slipped his hands under her buttocks, the whole of her trembling. Held her in place as he sucked on the tight little nub at the centre of her and relished her second scream of the evening, this time his name sung to the room.

There was no time now for him to wait, every part of him frayed and overheating. He had to be inside her. He'd spill himself on the sheets like a teenager if he wasn't, and soon. He reached for his bedside drawer, the condoms there. Sheathed himself with difficulty because he was affected by it too, this thing between them. Climbed over her and she wrapped her arms round him tight.

'Do you want me inside you?'

'Never more than now.'

'I'll go slowly,' he said, a promise voiced so he'd be forced to keep it, because all he wanted was to take. Ease his own agony. But tonight was for her. He kissed her, their tongues twining together, hot, erotic, as he slid against the folds of her, testing her wetness to ensure his entry would be easy enough, even though he wished he could promise her no pain. He notched himself at Hannah's centre, slid a bit further, a little way inside, and shut his eyes at the overwhelming pleasure of her heat enveloping only the tip of him. Worked gentle thrusts, a little deeper, deeper still, till Hannah's kisses became harder, more insistent. Bruising. She tilted her hips and he slid all the way inside, the hitch of her breath catching as he did so. He pulled his head back to look at her, to breathe through the pleasure to ensure her own, almost losing himself to his own orgasm right there.

'Good?' Sentences were beyond him, but he needed to check on her, the desire to make sure she wasn't hurting, that she was enjoying this, clasping at something deep inside him.

She opened her eyes and stared deep into his. Alessio's muscles trembled as she clenched tight and hot round him. Gripping him like the warmest silken glove, so tight it was almost his undoing.

'Perfect.' Her voice was a sigh shivering right through him. The pleasure threaded in her voice, like a plea.

'Should I move?'

'Move? Yes.'

His arms rested either side of her head. He stroked his thumbs to her temples, the necklace glittering in the soft light of the room, winding the blissful fantasy of the night round him once more.

'It would be my greatest pleasure.'

He rocked into her again and her eyes fluttered shut for a moment before opening. Holding his gaze. He said it would be his greatest pleasure, but all he craved was hers. She wrapped her legs tight round him, moving with him. He lost himself in her gaze, the flush of her skin, her lips, parted as if she couldn't take in enough air. Head thrown back and eyes glazed and far away with ecstasy. The heat of her, the scent of her around him. The sound of their bodies coming together wound him tighter and tighter. And the words left his mouth in his own language. Murmurings of ecstasy, of thanks, of truth.

'I don't understand,' she whispered, her blinks long and slow, her body tightening even harder round his. The tingle at the base of his spine heralded that he was close, so close.

And against all his better judgement he told her.

'You are so beautiful. It is too much. The privilege of being inside you.'

He changed his angle, went deeper. Ground his hips against her body. Her eyes widened as the bright spill of tears gleamed and threatened. Then her gaze became unfocused as she stiffened, gasped and cried out his name as she came. He plunged over the edge with her, the ecstasy tearing up his spine as if he were being struck by lightning. A blinding white flash in his head almost obliterated his consciousness. Then, as he came back to himself once the spasms subsided, all he could see was her. Tears now tracking from the corners of her eyes. The sparkling necklace at her throat. For tonight he'd allow them both the fantasy.

'La mia principessa.'

My princess.

Reality would come soon enough.

CHAPTER SEVEN

HANNAH SAT IN an armchair opposite Alessio's desk as he paced the rich crimson carpet of his office, checking his watch. He was dressed today in a crisp white shirt with a vibrant lemon-yellow tie. No jacket, which she suspected counted almost as casual with him. His body was tense, every part of him bristling as he almost wore a path through the plush flooring. She wanted to put her arm on him. To tell him it was okay to simply stop. She knew he could. That he could channel his restless energy elsewhere. How she craved a repeat performance. To spend her days and nights learning about him in every way. A slide of heat wound through her, hot and tempting. She didn't know how he could be so immune to it all, when she wanted to melt into a human-shaped puddle in her seat.

His gaze rested on her, cool and hard. So unlike the loose, relaxed, passionate man from the night before she was almost forced to wonder

whether she'd dreamt what had happened between them. Today all she saw was the ruler
of Lasserno, as if the man, Alessio Arcuri, had
ceased to exist.

'The hospital visit is private. No press have
been alerted. I hope you recognise the privilege
of this invitation. The children—'

*'The children are not in some circus where you
can watch them perform.* I'm aware how vulnerable children can be.'

She'd never use sick children as fodder, he
had to realise that. Or perhaps he didn't really
know her at all. But it wasn't about his comment. No, he was distancing himself from her.
Pulling away from the night they'd shared. This
morning, waking to a cold and empty bed. The
loss something almost palpable, drawing tears
to her eyes when she'd wanted to portray herself
as a sophisticate who understood they'd had one
night together and that was all it could ever be.

'Sex has a way of changing things...'

He'd warned her and he'd been right. She understood passion now, the bruising agony of it,
whereas once it had been an abstract concept experienced by others. Now, to her, Alessio sprang
to life in glorious colour. She knew how his body

worked in ways more than the cold anatomy of him. How his muscles bunched as he moved over her. The way the cords of his neck tensed as he was close, the blissful lack of focus in his eyes as he lost himself in her body. His care *for* her and her pleasure. All these things she could see even now, as his back was to her. They ran through her head, causing the whole of her to run hot, as if on fire. Things which showed he was a human and not the myth he tried so hard to portray to the world.

Yet something about the way she was being dismissed slashed at her deep inside. Though she supposed Alessio could hardly ask *are you okay?* if he wanted to keep what they'd done secret, given Stefano was sitting in the corner with one eyebrow cocked, watching them both. Did he know what had happened? Was it painted all over her face in the heat rising there? How was she going to keep things together at the hospital?

She took a deep breath. She was an adult, a grown woman. Last night had been a blissful, incredible, earth-shattering experience which could never be repeated. *One night. One night.* She'd say that mantra till it sank in and wove itself into the fibre of her being.

Stefano announced the cars were ready and they left, Alessio travelling alone. He always seemed alone, she realised, and perhaps that was the way it had to be as a ruler, a solitary journey. The ache of that burned in her chest as they arrived at the hospital to a back entrance with no fanfare. Hannah was introduced and welcomed as the official portrait artist, reminding her that this was her *job*, so she pulled out her sketch pad and her pencils from a satchel, the familiar weight of them in her hands spreading a calm through her.

Most people at the hospital seemed to be non-plussed with a prince in their midst, as if he did this often. Maybe he did, though it surprised her that the children's ward was such a dour place. White walls, grey floors. A few faded pictures on the wall. All the children tucked neatly into the beds, though a few brightened up when Alessio arrived, grinning at him, waving as if he were an old friend. He grinned back, greeted some by name. She turned to the doctor who'd brought them here.

'They seem to know him.'

The doctor smiled. 'Yes. A few of the children have serious health problems and have been here for some time. His Highness is popular with them. He visits as often as his schedule allows. He's planning works on the children's ward soon and likes to hear their ideas.'

Alessio talked to a sad-looking little boy wearing a cast. The soft concern on his face made him seem unrecognisable from the stern Prince in the palace he'd shown to her earlier.

'Have you thought about art on the walls?'

'We have hopes for many things. A complete refurbishment. So little money has been spent for so long. But the children would benefit if this were a happier place.'

Alessio now seemed to be having an intense conversation with another child's bear. It could have been a political discussion the way he gesticulated, whilst the little girl who owned the bear giggled, brightening the mood of the room. Hannah's heart melted at the scene, a small shred of joy in this joyless place.

'The corridor on the way in would be a wonderful place for a mural. If the children were being brought into the ward, it could make them less fearful to have something fun to look at. And then in here—' Hannah gestured to another blank wall, the ideas flowing as to the scenes she'd like to paint, the cartoon characters, the animals '—even bright paint colours would be a simple solution. I could jot down some colour schemes and ideas that don't cost much money if murals won't fit into the budget.'

'Please do.' The doctor smiled. 'Now I should introduce His Highness to some of the newest patients here. *Scusi.*'

Hannah sat in a plastic chair, far enough away so she had a perfect view of the whole room. She opened her sketch pad, lingering for a few moments on the drawing of Alessio's hands. His questing fingers, the way they drifted across her skin. But those were thoughts she wasn't allowed to have because there'd be no repeat of the night before. She ignored the ember glowing deep inside, one she couldn't stoke to life again. Instead, she turned to a fresh page and began another drawing. This picture was of Alessio, holding an animated conversation with the little girl's bear.

As she sketched the scene she became aware of movement nearby. She turned to a young boy who'd crept up beside her as she drew. Hannah smiled.

'Hello. What's your name?'

The boy's eyes widened, and she realised he

might not be able to speak English. She pulled out her phone and searched for a translation app. *'Come ti chiami?'*

He laughed, probably at her parlous pronunciation. 'Giulio.'

'Hello, Giulio. My name is Hannah.' She patted her chest.

He gave a tentative smile, then pointed to the page where she'd sketched Alessio. She didn't know what to say. Their barrier was language, but her art spoke a language all of its own. Hannah turned to another fresh page and considered the blank wall and what kind of mural she'd put there, then began sketching.

'Watch,' she said to the dark-eyed waif, who'd now pulled up a little plastic child's chair to sit beside her. And she drew a field of grass and flowers. A teddy bear's picnic, with all the kinds of fairy-tale foods the children might love. Ice cream, incredible towers of jelly, cakes. Not a vegetable to be seen. Bears playing, flying kites, including one which had been blown away on a strong gust of wind, and the bear holding it sailing into the sky with others trying to pull it down.

The little boy next to her laughed, and the

sound spurred her on. She began mapping out a few ideas, losing herself in the fun of creating a joyous space, something better than this, something to make the children less fearful. Soon she had a small audience watching her. Children with wide eyes and wider smiles. What more could she draw for them? She didn't really watch television, didn't go to see movies, and had no nieces and nephews, being an only child, so wasn't sure what children liked. That sense of isolation pricked at her. Most of the time she didn't really feel lonely, not with her art. It was as if she were always in the presence of the person whose portrait she painted. Immersed in them, kept company by their picture and her understanding of them as a person. Today, she was overwhelmed by the knowledge there was only her. She looked up at Alessio, talking to some of the nurses. He was alone too. Did he ever have the sense of it, a kind of emptiness, or did duty fill the spaces?

He glanced over in her direction, almost like he knew she was watching him. As he took in the children surrounding her, a look crossed his face. Something intense, not implacable at all. The potency of that moment ignited those flickering embers deep inside. Then a child touched her arm and pointed at the page. She laughed because she knew they wanted her to keep drawing, so she turned her attention to the sketch pad once more. Alessio wasn't safe. The children were. Looking at the boy who'd first come to her, with his dark curls and eyes, Hannah began to sketch him, a little caricature. It was how she had first started with her art. Doodling in class, drawing friends, till her parents had died and the obsession overtook her, that her memory of their faces might fade. So she'd drawn them incessantly, etching them into her brain so she would never forget.

A shadow crossed her page as she was almost done. A shiver of awareness shimmied down her spine. There was only one person it could be.

'You have a crowd.' Alessio's voice was as warm as the summer's day outside, heating her as if she'd stepped into the midday sunshine.

She tore herself from her drawings and their gazes caught and held. Her pulse took off at a gallop, the wild beat only for him. 'Is your ego coping with the lack of attention?'

He did nothing for a heartbeat, then burst out laughing. It was as if happiness had exploded into the room. Everyone stared at him. The princely Alessio was a foreboding force. The passionate man in bed a study in absolute focus. But *this* man, laughing and real, showing his human side for the first time since she'd known him—this man was a danger. The type of man who could break a woman's heart.

Except there was nothing left to break. She'd lost her heart years ago on the day she'd lost everything. She'd encased it in a protective cage and now nothing could get through to harm it ever again. Hannah ignored those musings, and simply took in the man smiling at her in his own blinding way.

'You're a woman who's hard for my ego every day. But I'm sensible enough to know who the real talent is here. It's not me.'

'It's not me either—it's the health professionals.'

The burnt umber of his eyes smouldered like brown coal on fire as the look on his face softened, darkened. She knew it well, having seen it in his bedroom the night before. A shiver of longing coursed through her. Her cheeks heated as she remembered the pleasure, the delicious aches which remained. The memory of Alessio and his body over her. Inside her. Did it show on her face? Because naked desire was written all over his. But it had only been for one night. They'd agreed, and, as much as she craved more of him, she knew she'd only take what life gave her rather than ask for more. Since in the main, if she wanted more, life slapped her down in the cruellest possible ways.

'They are indeed. What are you doing there?' He nodded to the pages on which she'd drawn.

'I had some ideas to brighten up the ward, make it a more welcoming place for the children.'

The doctor who'd spoken to her earlier approached. 'Signorina Barrington suggested some murals. As you know, Your Highness, we talked of the ward becoming more welcoming. Less clinical.'

Alessio glanced at his watch, at Stefano, who began to approach. 'That's an excellent idea. I'll ensure there's a place in the budget. Anything for the children.'

He crouched down on his haunches. Said something to the children surrounding her. A slightly older boy answered back.

'Do you know any superheroes?' Alessio asked.

Hannah smiled. 'I'm sure I can think of a few. Does he want me to draw some?'

Alessio nodded. Even in this position, he ruled the room like the Prince he was. His gaze dropped to her mouth and lingered there. His lips parted as if he was going to say something more, but no words came. Those perfectly drawn lips of his had spent the night exploring her body in the most exquisite of ways, finding places she didn't know could give her pleasure. Yet Alessio had seemed to find them all.

'I—I should get started, then.'

She scribbled on the page with shaky fingers. The children seemed enthralled, and she was too, but by the man blazing in front of her. His nostrils flared. Did he know what she was thinking about? Was he thinking the same? It couldn't go anywhere, so better not to dwell on it at all.

They held each other like that for a few moments, their gazes clashing. Then Stefano approached and cleared his throat. Alessio stood, the break between them almost more painful than waking this morning to find herself alone.

'We should go. You have a meeting with the Health Minister.'

It was said in English for her benefit, she was

sure. The children clamoured around Alessio as he moved to leave, making obvious noises of disappointment as they were ushered back to bed by the staff. All Hannah could do was watch his back as he walked away from her, as if she'd ceased to exist.

Alessio walked through the maze-like corridors of the hospital exquisitely aware of the woman trailing behind him, whom he could feel as if she were touching him. The flush on her cheeks. Her wide eyes. Those lips of hers a cherry blush. She had the look of a woman well-loved, as if she'd suddenly come into herself.

It had been all he could do to leave his bed this morning. To gather his clothes, the evidence they'd been together. To shower, scrub his body and try to wash her away. Yet he had failed. Nothing could wash away the memory of her sighs, her skin, so soft under his fingers.

Then with the children… How they'd flocked to her, her natural charm and grace drawing them in like the sunshine on a spring day, something beautiful and warm, welcoming. In a pretty blue dress with dark hair spilling unrestrained over her shoulders, she looked like every fantasy drawn to life. For those fleeting moments in her presence he didn't see problems, but possibilities, where his life only had one course. Right now he should let her join Stefano in the car behind his and travel to the palace by himself. Yet he was tired. Tired of the feeling his journey was one which should always be taken alone, with no one to share it with. For a moment he allowed himself to want without guilt.

'Signorina Barrington comes with me. I wish to know more about her ideas for the children's ward.'

'Do I need to ask again?' Stefano murmured. *Do you know what you're doing?*

Alessio cut him off. 'No.'

The word left his mouth with barely a thought, and once uttered he would not take it back. He never did. Yet the truth screamed loud in his head. He didn't know what he was doing. He should be far away from her. Travelling with her was a breach of a self-imposed protocol.

And right now, he didn't care.

Stefano gave a small bow, the merest of smiles on his face. His eyebrow rose a fraction once more, the expression of amusement seeming to have become almost a permanent fixture Alessio had seen it so often over the past days. He wouldn't explain because none of this was explicable. His driver opened the door of the car and Hannah slipped into the back seat with him. Clipped on her seatbelt and looked out of the window. The car slid away from the rear of the hospital, starting the journey towards the palace.

'You were wonderful with the kids,' Hannah said, her voice soft and almost wistful.

'So were you.' They'd flocked to her, with her drawings of them, cartoon characters and everything in between. Those unwell children giggling with delight at the things she drew.

'They're an easy audience.'

Her smile lit up the interior of the car. Something in his chest clenched, the whole of him too hot and tight. They'd agreed on one night, that it was enough, yet he hadn't realised one night with her could *never* be enough. There was nothing experienced about her, but Hannah's innocence and naked enthusiasm were like a drug that had him craving. He might never erase the memories from his room, which seemed ridiculous, yet no other woman had ever graced his bed at the palace. He dreaded the anticipation of lonely nights when she left. Craving to take his fill now, whilst he could.

His palms itched, wanting to touch, determined not to. Yet his resolve failed as she kept speaking. All he thought about was her natural beauty and how the children clambered over her as if she were a pied piper. As if she were some kind of saviour.

'There are so many ways you could help them. A mural would be a beautiful addition to the ward. It would brighten their lives, especially the little ones who need to stay there a long time. I have so many ideas.'

The cabin of the vehicle closed in on him, compressing to a pinpoint that was only them, as if the rest of the world didn't exist. He loosened his tie, now too tight round his neck. He needed to get out of this small space so he could breathe, so he could think. Even the journey back to the palace felt too long. And, since there was a driver up front, there was nothing he could do here. Yet he kept a small office in the capital, a well-guarded secret, and they were only minutes away from it.

'Manuel, please take us to the city office.'

'Of course, Your Highness.'

A few deviations and they arrived, driving

through a gated archway and into an internal courtyard. The car stopped and Alessio didn't wait for his driver. He opened the door himself and stepped out into the baking summer's heat.

Hannah frowned. 'Are you leaving?'

He peered into the cabin where she sat, her teeth biting into her bottom lip. 'No. We have things to discuss. I have an office. It's private.'

Her mouth opened but she didn't reply. Merely nodded and followed him from the car. The few staff who ran the premises in his absence scrambled as he entered unannounced. He smiled at them, but it felt more rictus than genuine, each second not alone with Hannah a moment wasted. With introductions over he flung back the door of his office, and she followed him inside. He closed it behind her. Stood in the cool silence and could breathe again.

'What do you want to discuss, Your Highness?'

He wheeled around, hating that this formality had returned. He'd been wrong in the way he'd treated her this morning. Especially when the desire still ran rich and hot through his veins, calling him out as a liar for pretending what had happened between them was nothing. And, whilst he might lie to himself, he couldn't lie to her.

'Is once enough for you?'

Hannah's eyes darkened, pupils black in the oceanic green. He'd seen them look the same as she'd come apart underneath him in his bed, beautiful and wide with desire matching his own. Her lips parted as a flush crept from her throat. 'Never.'

'Good, because I want more.' His voice was a hiss through clenched teeth at the agony of need unfulfilled. More a command than a request. Harsh and low. Clotted with desire.

Who stepped first, he couldn't have said. They fell into each other, his hands thrust into her silken locks of hair. Lips on hers, hard and fast. She clung to his shoulders, their tongues touching, and he moved back to a large sofa in the corner. Dropped into it with her straddling his hips, rocking forward on the hardness of him as he groaned into her mouth. He slid his hands to her buttocks, drawing her even closer, hiking up the skirt of her dress till he could grab at the soft, pale skin of her thighs. She quivered under his palms as he moved back in the seat a little and slid a finger between them, her underwear damp with evidence of her arousal. He rubbed over her most sensitive spot. Light touches that had her panting and squirming against him, holding her on a cruel edge. Tormenting her in the way she had unknowingly tormented him by merely existing, the noises she made increasingly desperate. He didn't care. He wanted her to beg for her pleasure, here in his office, where they could both lose their minds.

He was agonisingly hard now. Her heat was against him, relentless and brutal. He'd been unprepared. He had no protection. The pulse of need drove him on, but as much as he craved to release himself and slide into the wet heat of her, he wouldn't. The risk to her as much as to him was too great. This journey could lead nowhere permanent. But pleasure was something they could give one another. He had nothing on this afternoon he couldn't cancel. They could spend it in his rooms once back at the palace, or in hers. It didn't matter, so long as he was inside her.

Hannah let out a groan. A curse. A *plea.*

'Ah, *bella*. Am I neglecting you?' The words were said against her gasping mouth. He slid two fingers inside her, curled them to reach the sensitive spot he knew drove her wild. Worked his thumb over the tight bundle of nerves at the juncture of her thighs as her breath held, the whole of her drawn tight as a bow till she broke apart around him, her shuddering body letting him know she'd tumbled over the edge, moaning his name as her spasms went on and on, clenching round his fingers. With a final flutter she sagged into him. He withdrew from her, wrapped Hannah tight in his arms. His own body, so hard and aching, objected to the way she nestled into him, screaming for its own release. Yet he did nothing, giving her this time. After a few moments relaxed in his arms she stirred, rocked against him again. He gasped as a bright burst of pleasure exploded through him.

'What about you?' Her voice was a sigh against his neck, feathering over his skin. She pulled back, her eyes soft, dreamy. Skin flushed a delicate pink. Mouth plump and well-kissed.

What he wouldn't give to forget being a prince, forget the consequences, take for himself and be damned. But that would make him like his father, and he was not that man.

'I didn't come prepared for this.'

'You wouldn't make a very good boy scout, then, would you?'

He chuckled, even though the ache in his groin

intensified as she voiced her need to give him pleasure as well. Too often people had been prepared to take from him. Someone considering his true desires seemed like hedonism at its finest.

'It's something I've never considered. Being Prince of Lasserno, others tend to prepare for me.'

The corners of her plush, kiss-reddened lips curled into a wicked smile. She leaned forward, her voice a whisper in his ear. 'Luckily I have a few ideas for how I can help, *Your Highness.*'

A quake ran through him at the sound of his title spoken with her low, intent voice. It was almost a taunt but he didn't care. She pulled back, and with trembling fingers Hannah worked at his belt buckle, the closure on his trousers, the zip. Then her cool hand reached into his underwear and took him out. He stifled a groan. Almost lost control in that moment, unable to tear his gaze away as she tightened her grip and worked him the way he'd shown her the night before. Damn, if they weren't going to make a mess here and right now, but he didn't care. Gone mad with a feverish desire that nothing bar her would satisfy. Then Hannah moved from his lap, dropped to her knees on the floor before him. Loosened the relentless grip and stroking which had him close to the edge and almost tumbling over.

'I don't really know what I'm doing—you'll have to guide me.'

Alessio frowned, not sure what she was talking about until she dropped her head, and the warmth of her breath caressed a sliver of flesh at his stomach. He jerked in her hand as the knowledge of what she was about to do coursed through him like an electric current.

'Devour me like you've never been hungrier in your life,' he groaned.

She looked up at him, eyes that intense rock-pool green, dark and still. With depths he could never fathom. A wicked smile played at the corners of her perfect mouth. 'Just remember, I'm not going to stop.'

She took him into the heat of her mouth. His brain blanked with white noise roaring in his ears. Hannah was tentative till he moaned, and her efforts became intense. Determined. His hand tangled into her hair, guiding her, but there was no need. She followed his instructions to a perfection belying her inexperience. He was close, so close, feeling the tingling at the base of his spine, the heaviness, the tightening in his groin. He held on but the vision of her worshipping him like this, because that was how it seemed, drove him to the edge of control. She wanted him as much as he wanted her. Of that, he had no doubt. And her words, *'I'm not going to stop...'* ran on repeat. Like an endless loop in his head, winding him tighter and higher.

'Hannah… I'm going to… Hannah…'

He tugged at her hair in warning, but she didn't let up on the relentless rhythm. For once in his life he allowed the scorching fire of his orgasm tear through his body with no thought or care for the consequences.

Letting the burn set him free.

CHAPTER EIGHT

ALESSIO SAT BEHIND his desk, trying and failing to make sense of some financial reports. The numbers on the page swirled and blurred into one another. Yesterday had been an exercise in hedonism. Something he'd never indulged in. He and Hannah in his city office. Cancelling his appointments. Spending the afternoon in bed, repaying her a thousand-fold, making her scream. That filled his thoughts. Not these dry figures and graphs about tourism which should be holding his interest.

Yet he couldn't see what he and Hannah were doing as a mistake. Not now. It might be a glorious folly, like the pavilion on the palace grounds. Built to a love that was all an illusion. But they had set an end: the date Hannah left Lasserno. Then he could choose his princess, establish his throne. Renew the glory of his country.

Still, what had once driven him now held no excitement. He rubbed his hands over his face.

Took another long draught of his coffee. Today it was as if his bones were made of lead. Strange that around Hannah he seemed…lighter. More energised, invigorated, as if plugged straight into a power source. Not bowed by this weight, as if the expectations of the world sat on his shoulders.

He checked the time, then his diary. More meetings. Soon Stefano would walk in and they'd go. Instead of preparing, all he could think about was another evening in bed with Hannah. Driving away his worries for Lasserno in the warmth of her body. The way her hands stroked tenderly over his skin. A shred of softness at the end of a hard day…

'Sir, His Highness is busy… Sir! You can't go—'

'My abdication does not mean this has ceased to be my palace. I go where I choose. I choose to see my son.'

Alessio's blood froze, then his repressed rage heated it till it was near boiling. That voice sent a jagged spear through the heart of him. His father. Since his abdication he'd barely been near the palace, holed up in his personal villa on the outskirts of the capital, where few people paid any attention to his exploits and greater excesses. The double doors of his office were flung open and the former Prince himself strode in as if he still owned the room. To some people in this country he still did, but that was a problem for another day. Stefano followed, fists clenched.

'I'm sorry—'

Alessio held up his hand. If he'd not been able to curb his father, then his best friend had no chance. 'It's okay. I'm sure he'll leave soon.'

The man in question looked around the room as Stefano backed out and closed the doors behind him. The corner of his father's top lip curled in a sneer. 'I don't favour what you've done with the place.'

'I don't care. Your taste isn't mine.' In *anything*. He'd happily rid the space of the more garish furniture and installed less frivolous antique pieces, more solid and befitting the future ruler of Lasserno.

Alessio gritted his teeth so hard he could almost taste blood. This was the man who'd left his wife and Lasserno's beloved Princess to die alone. The man who'd plundered the crown jewels as he'd seen fit, as if it wasn't bad enough in days long past that the royal family had lost the coronation ring present in so many portraits here, never to be recovered. A reminder to Alessio of responsibility and all he was tasked to protect.

'All your talk of austerity and yet you decide to redecorate. I wonder, is this what hypocrisy looks like?'

'This furniture was already in the palace. None of it's new. At least I didn't raid the crown jewels, the *country's* treasures, to fund my lifestyle or provide baubles to sycophants.'

His father threw back his head and laughed. Dressed in a favoured Savile Row suit, he remained a handsome man, although his hair was greying, and he carried a little thickness around the middle. To Alessio's disgust, he looked more like this man than he did his beautiful mother, with her pale hair and eyes. His father's genes had erased everything of his mother from him… almost. Not her inherent goodness, he hoped. Alessio strove to carry that always.

'The country's? No. We're an absolute monarchy. Everything in Lasserno is *ours*, to take as we see fit. Or have you forgotten? Next, you'll be talking constitutions and presidents. Save me from a straw crown. I want none of it.'

Alessio sat still in his seat, the lessons of his

childhood coming to the fore, when all he wanted was to stand and rage. But he refused to give this man the satisfaction of showing any emotion. Anyhow, toddler tantrums were his father's specialty. He had more control. Alessio gripped the arms of his chair a little tighter, to prevent himself from leaping from it.

'A ruler can be absolute, and still do the right thing by the country and its people.'

'Doing what's right for oneself is much more entertaining. Yet, despite your efforts, *the people* don't seem to think you're doing a good job. What are the press saying again?'

That he was cold. Autocratic. Opaque. Those words might have stung if his path weren't clear. The people would see, once Lasserno took its rightful place on the world stage rather than being a forgotten backwater.

'I don't care, and that's where our core difference lies. Since I'm a busy man fixing the messes you left, get to the point. Why did you come here? I suspect it wasn't to criticise my decorating style.'

His father took a seat in the chair opposite Alessio's desk, lounging in an indolent kind of way that was the man's specialty.

'I've come to congratulate you.' His father's gloating tone sounded a warning. 'You're not a lost cause yet, when for some time I thought you were all work and no play. She really is a masterstroke.'

Alessio froze. It couldn't be. He *couldn't* know about Hannah. Everyone in the palace was faithful to him. No one would say a thing. He'd learned a hard lesson about misplaced trust and had rid himself of his father's cronies and hangers-on the minute the man had walked away from the throne. Any whispers could only be rumour because he'd been seen with a woman, whose presence had been well reported before she'd even arrived in Lasserno. It was one of the few things he'd allowed Stefano to tell the press, the coup of his coronation portrait being painted by the world's finest young artist, something to be celebrated rather than hidden.

'Who are you talking about?'

His father waved his hand theatrically, twisting that spear even harder. His disdain for his son and only child had seemed to increase over the years. Alessio had long ceased trying to impress the man. He'd given up around the time he'd been called home from England, leaving behind his dreams of riding for his country any more. Arriving home to find Lasserno in disarray.

'The artist. I should have done the same.'

Alessio's veins turned to ice. 'Stop talking in riddles.'

Yet even as he said the words his voice was like dust in his mouth, dry and lacking conviction. His father was a master of playing vicious, wicked games. He enjoyed them, and Alessio wondered whether the 'mistake' in Hannah's placement at his table for dinner hadn't been a mistake at all but a move designed to create gossip.

'Installed my mistress before marriage. What did that prim little English nanny of yours always say? Something about beginning as you mean to end things.'

Start as you mean to finish.

'I have no mistress.' That was not what was happening here. Hannah would be leaving soon. But the denial caught in his throat, threatening to throttle him.

His father was only guessing, assuming his son would debauch any beautiful young woman the same as he would. The bile rose in Alessio's throat. He tried not to think that was exactly what he was doing. This was different. He didn't have a wife; he didn't have a child. There was nothing currently tying him to any person. He was as free as he could be.

'You can keep telling that to your conscience. Marry the perfect ice-cold princess and have your passionate piece already installed. You're setting the expectations of your wife early. Perfect.'

'I have nothing to trouble my conscience. Unlike you, I'll be a faithful husband and I would never leave my wife to die alone.'

'Your mother wanted me nowhere near her, especially not at the end. If she had I might have spent more time with her. Let's say she was satisfied with having an heir. She was never going to give me a spare. Trust me when I say a lack of passion makes for a very cold bed to lie in for eternity.'

Alessio stood then, began pacing the carpet.

'Perhaps if you'd been faithful, she might have been inclined to like you rather than despise you. Take care. This is my *mother* whose memory you're disparaging.'

'Whose necklace you allowed your little artist to wear. Which was sensible. They form no part of the crown jewels. Sets the girl's expectations, wearing secondary gems. She'll always know her place.'

'She is not my anything.'

'Lie to yourself all you want but say it with more conviction next time. Or better, admit to your failings. You have me as a father after all. One day you'll awaken a lonely old man and only then, when it's too late, you'll see I was right.'

'Is that all you have to say?' Alessio gritted his teeth, tried to maintain his temper. Swept his hands over the paperwork sitting on the desk. 'Because I have work, and no time for your ravings. You chose to abdicate this responsibility. Now leave me be.'

'Of course, *Your Highness.*' His father's voice was a cold sneer. 'Just remember, the work is always there. As the English like to say, *All work and no play makes Alessio a dull boy.* My suggestion? Keep your artist and find your royal wife. What use is being a prince if you can't have what you want?'

His father rose with the presence of a ruler, stalked to the study doors and flung them back. They smacked into the walls on either side with unnecessary force as he left the room. Alessio couldn't stop moving, the anger burning in his gut as he paced. His father didn't really know what was going on—he was fishing for information. But this, the palace, all the intrigue…it would sully what he had with Hannah, their last precious days spent together. He wanted perfect memories for them both. Had to get her away from here, but everywhere was fraught. Any of the other royal homes, the royal yacht, had bigger problems. Whilst he'd rid the palace in the capital of his father's sycophants, he couldn't be sure of elsewhere.

Where to go? Somewhere close enough to the capital to be able to return easily, but far enough away to avoid prying eyes.

Stefano entered the room, brow furrowed in concern. 'All okay?'

In those days after his father's abdication, only his best friend knew the true extent of the trouble his father had caused. Alessio stilled. The solution stood in front of him. One he'd used a few times before when riding his horses had ceased to be enough. 'I need to escape for a few days. The usual way.'

Stefano nodded, yet his eyebrows rose again. 'Will Hannah be joining you?'

'Yes.' Alessio clenched his jaw. He would have no judgement on this, not from his friend. 'Are you going to ask whether I know what I'm doing?'

Stefano gave him a wry smile. This man was one of his closest supporters. Like a brother. He placed a hand on Alessio's shoulder and gave a brief squeeze of solidarity.

'I don't have to, my friend. I think you know exactly what you're doing. And for once it's what you want to do, rather than what you believe you should. That's a *good* thing.'

Stefano released him and left the room, phone to his ear. In his office, all alone with the weight of his ancestors' portraits around him, Alessio wasn't sure he could take any comfort from his friend's parting words.

CHAPTER NINE

HANNAH WALKED DOWN a gangplank to the harbour at dawn. The whole journey had been cloaked in secrecy. She had been told to pack for the beach for two days, and that was it. Not that she'd come to Lasserno prepared for needing beachwear. When she'd told Alessio, a host of bags had arrived in her room. Clothes with tags from designers who left her breathless, so she simply stuffed it all into a duffel bag she'd brought with her. In the pale morning light Alessio looked nothing like his usual self, unrecognisable in shorts showing off his strong calves, a T-shirt, cap jammed on his head, like a disguise. The whole episode was all subterfuge. He'd even driven them here through a back exit of the palace, with no entourage. Something cloak and dagger about it thrilled her.

They arrived at a magnificent yacht that looked as if it had come straight out of a classic movie, with three soaring masts and gleaming, honeyed wood. Alessio helped her aboard, where they were met by the crew. He shook their hands. Introduced her.

'Remember, the same rules as last time,' Alessio said.

The captain nodded. 'Of course, sir. We'll be underway immediately.'

'Thank you.'

No *Your Highness*…no bowing. Little ceremony at all, as someone spirited away their bags. Alessio slid a hand to the small of her back and they traversed the expansive deck to the bow. As they reached the rail, Alessio checked his watch. She placed her hand over his wrist.

'You do that constantly.'

'I want to see if we're leaving in good time.'

He'd told her this weekend was for them, to get away. It seemed as if he never could, always managing his day to the last second. She turned his wrist over, unclipped the burnished gold band and slid the timepiece from his wrist. Rubbed a thumb over his pulse-point. Over the mark the clasp had left. Relishing the feel of his smooth, golden skin under her fingers.

'You need to stop sometimes.' She clasped the watch in her fist as Alessio let out a slow breath, his shoulders relaxing as if some weight had been removed. 'I'd like to pitch it into the sea to make sure you do, but it's probably valuable.'

'My maternal grandfather gave it to me.'

'Did you like him?'

The corner of Alessio's mouth kicked up into a smile. 'I did.'

'Then I'll keep it safe.' She slipped it into the pocket of her skirt, its weight against her thigh. A reminder of how little time they had, which was something she shouldn't even be thinking about. She should be living in the now, because her time here had always had an end date. Hannah tipped her head back to look up into the complicated rigging.

'This is an amazing boat.'

'*Il Delfino*. A schooner built in 1910. One hundred and seventy feet long, if you're interested.'

'It's beautiful.'

'So are you.'

She smiled, breath catching in her throat. 'Thank you.'

Since her parents had died, there'd been no one to tell her she was beautiful. Her dad had said those words to her, to her mother, all the time. Back then her parents had made sure she felt as attractive as an awkward teen could, with pimples and hormones causing trouble. On the other hand, her aunt and uncle hadn't realised what she'd needed. Or hadn't cared. Maybe the only thing they'd ever been interested in was the money her parents had left.

Tears burned at her eyes. There was no time for them here. Instead she stared out over the horizon. Ribbons of pink and gold threaded through the sky. The cool breeze brushed her face.

Alessio moved behind her, wrapping strong arms round her body. She leaned into him, tried to relax. To make the most of every second here.

'This feels like another movie moment,' she said.

'Is that a bad thing this time?'

'Only if the boat sinks.'

'She's had a complete refit, if you're worried.'

Hannah wasn't. Around Alessio she almost felt more secure than with anyone else, apart from the way she had as a child with her mother and father. 'I'm sure you'll keep me safe.'

His arms tightened a fraction. She closed her eyes to savour the moment. He'd keep her safe physically. Emotionally though…it was as if she stood in a crowded room, naked. But this, between them, was *all* physical. An attraction. Nothing more.

'You mentioned something to the crew about rules,' she said. 'What are they?'

'This is Stefano's yacht. Here, I'm not the Prince of Lasserno, I'm him.'

He played Stefano, so he could hide her. Part of that made sense. He was protecting them both from the press. Another part of it stung like a bee ruining a barefoot walk in the grass.

'Stefano? This isn't just any old boat. Where did he get it?'

'Family. Stefano's the Conte di Varno. The Moretti family and mine have a long history. Each count has served the royal family in their own way. Stefano's way is as my private secretary, since I trust him implicitly.'

'It's nice that you have so much trust in someone.'

Alessio loosened his arms and turned her, a slight frown forming on his brow, the look concerned and earnest. 'And you don't?'

It was as if she were standing on a precipice. This between them was supposed to be casual. That meant light banter and fun. But she was driven to unburden herself, as if telling Alessio might set herself free.

'My uncle was a financial advisor. He looked after my inheritance. Six months ago, he ignored my wishes. Invested in something I didn't want. That investment failed. My parents didn't have much, but my dad had an insurance policy. It's all gone now. I'm hanging on to the cottage.'

Barely. Hannah didn't know if it felt any better, having told Alessio. It was a terrible admission, her failure to keep an eye on things.

Alessio's jaw hardened. His mouth a tight, thin line.

'Are the police involved? Surely by law, your uncle wasn't allowed to do such a thing?'

She hated this. Hated that the people who should have been looking after her interests had let her down so badly. Whilst they hadn't been her parents, they'd been her last link to one of them. But she'd learned a powerful lesson from the experience. All she really had was herself.

'He used a few people's money, and he shouldn't have.' He'd been so sure that everything would be okay, and that in the end she'd thank him for ignoring her wishes. The arrogance of it. 'And yes, the police are involved.

But that won't get my funds back. Everything my parents left me, I lost.'

'Ah, *bella*. It's not your fault.' Alessio stepped forward and bundled her in his arms. She rested her head on his chest as he held her tight. As if he were holding her together. And all of it was dangerous. They weren't meant to share, not like this.

'Would you have taken this commission if your uncle hadn't done what he did?'

'No.' She pulled back. Shook her head, honesty all she had left. 'You. Horse riding. The showjumping circuit. It brings back memories I'd do anything to avoid. But now I'm here, I'm glad I agreed.'

'I'm…glad too.'

She noticed it, the slightest of hesitations in a man she suspected hesitated over nothing. He tightened his arms around her.

'Do you trust me?' he asked.

Hannah was lost in the deep, warm brown of his eyes. She didn't know if she trusted anyone, and that caused her gut to clench like a hard fist inside. She had to remind herself what this truly was. It had an end date marching up faster and faster. She'd pack her bags, her art equipment and leave. Paint his portrait. Throw all her emotion into it, then set it free and let him go. Alessio would find and marry his perfect princess, and all would once again be right with the world.

'With my body? I trust you implicitly.'

Alessio's smile in answer to her comment was sultry and slow.

'I'll always look after you.'

That sounded as if this had a permanence to it, which she knew to be untrue. But then, words were easy. It was actions which were harder. And she knew he wouldn't stop her winging away from here. He'd put her on the plane himself. But it was fine. She'd known the day her parents died that the picture of her own life would be different from what she'd imagined it would be as a child. In her wildest dreams, she'd never believed a fortnight like this could happen to her. And the memory of it would be enough. Would carry her through the years.

It *would.*

Enough of this introspective mood. The glorious sun rose in the sky, filling her with a lazy warmth. The tang of salt hung invigoratingly in the air. They had time and she'd take her fill of every second. She needed to lighten the mood, since it had become far too serious.

'So, this is Stefano's yacht. Don't you have one of your own?'

'Of course. Mine's a modern yacht. Some might say…better,' Alessio said with a smirk.

'And I bet it has a crown embossed on the bow.' She gave him a smile of her own. She liked him like this, the man relaxed, unlike the Prince he showed to the world every day.

He held out his arms. Even in casual clothes he had an intoxicating presence. As if he owned the world. 'What's being a prince if one doesn't have the crown?'

'Is your ego taking a bit of a battering that I might like Stefano's better than yours?'

'My ego remains intact, despite your best and most constant efforts.' Those wide arms of his wrapped round her again. Pulled her close. Dropped his head to her ear. 'Let me show you.'

His body pressed into hers, his arousal, bold and obvious, stoking the fire of her own. She flexed her hips against his hardness. Ran her hands down his back, relishing the strength of his muscles as they flexed under her fingers.

'I think there are a few things I need to know whilst I'm here,' she said.

'Port is left. Starboard is right.'

'Thank you, Your Highness.' Hannah laughed. 'No. Your talk of the rules before. Are there any I should know?'

Alessio looked up at the golden sky, brow furrowed as if in thought. 'The first rule is that I'm always right.'

'Oh, really? Any others?'

'Hmm… The second…' He tapped at his chin then looked down at her, the colour of his eyes swallowed by his pupils, the dawn painting him golden as well. 'When we're alone together you should always be naked. Clothes are a travesty on you.'

Heat rose to her cheeks. 'And is that rule reciprocated?'

'*Ovviamente.* Now we're heading out on water, rule two is invoked. You're wearing too many clothes.'

'Are you sure about that?' she asked as Alessio inched his fingers under her shirt, stroking the sensitive skin of her side. A shiver of goosebumps skittered down her arms. He began unbuttoning the soft cotton shirt she wore, his eyes glowing and intent. Always fierce. Always in a hurry, or at least where she was concerned. He dropped his head and began kissing her shoulder, light brushes that made her liquid in his arms.

'I refer you to rule number one,' he murmured, the warmth of his breath tickling her neck.

She laughed again, something so different about him here, out of the palace. As if he could become a man, rather than being a ruler of all he surveyed. She gave a little push on his chest and he let her go. She stood back. Shrugged her top from her shoulders, slowly exposing the exquisite floral bikini top she wore underneath from the clothes she'd been given. His gaze raked over her, jaw tight, arousal straining at his zipper.

'Dio. Sei così bella.'

She didn't know what that meant but it sounded like a worship, a benediction. Yet he stood there, fully clothed, simply watching her set the pace.

'Where's the reciprocation?'

The corner of his mouth curled into a heated smile.

'Come here,' he said, the voice all command that sent a shiver of longing through her. She loved this of him, the demanding, passionate man. All the while knowing that if she said no, if she took a step back, he'd wait for her.

'Still rule number one?'

He raised an imperious eyebrow, but a smile teased his mouth. She walked forward into his embrace, his lips sinking onto her own. She never failed to be surprised at how such a seemingly hard man could be all softness when he held her. As if the fact he had a human side was their secret.

'I'm not being a good host. It's time I showed you the stateroom.'

Alessio swung her into his arms and strode down the deck like a man bent on completing a mission—that of making her cry his name to the room.

Alessio woke to the lull of slapping water on the side of the yacht. The gentle sway of the ocean. For the first time in an age, he was at some kind of peace. Sleepy, sated. Barely caring whether he moved all day. There was one reason for this newfound satisfaction—a person. He reached to the side of the bed for Hannah and brushed only the warmth of empty sheets. Not long gone, then. He lay for a moment, listening for her, but there was no sound, so he rolled over and sat up, scraping his hand through his hair.

She was curled on a sofa opposite the bed at the other side of the room. Feet tucked under her. Drawing on a sketch pad on her lap with a stick of charcoal.

'You're naked,' he said. The sight of her perfect skin made the blood race down low. Would he ever get enough of her? He feared not.

She glanced up at him, the merest of smiles touching her well-kissed lips.

'Rule number two, remember?'

He lounged back on the bed. 'And you did what I said. Rule number one. It's a miracle.'

She snorted, such a cute sound, as she peered up at him again, then returned to the page before her. Sketching, rubbing at the paper with her fingers. 'I think I liked you better when you were asleep.'

'I don't believe you,' he said, his body heating each time her insightful gaze returned to him. Arousal, heavy and low, snaked through him again. This attraction, it overtook everything, an overwhelming need only Hannah could satisfy. 'You like me very much when I'm awake.'

He didn't hide how much she affected him.

He'd not hold anything back from her. The free-dom of such a short time frame meant he didn't have to. Yet the realisation of how little time they had left stung like a forgotten wound exposed to seawater. A surprising and unwelcome jolt. He ignored it. There were better ways of using their day than musing over things like that. He patted the bed next to him. 'Come here.'

'Does your ego need stroking?'

An insistent pulse of desire kept beating its demanding tempo. 'Something needs stroking.'

She didn't even look up at him, her focus all on the page, a slight frown creasing her brow. 'No. I haven't been doing enough sketching. You keep distracting me.'

Hannah being more interested in what was on the piece of paper in front of her than in the real man put him in his place, firmly rooted in a world where he was not the most desirable, sought-after person. It made him feel normal, feel *real*.

A blessed relief.

'Can I see what you're doing?'

'You get the final painting. Everything else is mine. Just lie back and enjoy it. Everyone needs to stop some time.' She looked up at him, that frown still present, her face a study of intensity, making him believe she saw all of him. His sins, his flaws. There was no hiding them with her. And it made him curious.

'What do you see when you look at me?'

'Do you really want to know?'

'I asked the question.'

She put down her charcoal. Placed her hand flat on the page in front of her so her drawing was hidden.

'You like to think you begin and end as Prince of Lasserno. That there's nothing else. But you're more.'

Inside of him, something clenched. Almost like a warning, but she'd piqued his interest now.

'Tell me.'

'Someone who works hard. Too hard.' A shaft of sunlight filtered through the cabin window, painting her pale skin in its warm glow. She looked a picture of perfection sitting there. Alessio didn't want the moment to end. He shrugged.

'It's all part of the job description. My father didn't work hard enough. Saw life as a prince for only what he could get from it. He almost drove Lasserno into ruin.' A tightness rose inside again. Of things unfinished, of work yet to do. It was relentless, exhausting. Never-ending. A needling sensation interrupted the moment. He raised his left wrist, but his watch wasn't there.

'I've put it away for a few days. You need to relax. You'll have plenty of time to save the country. Years of it, in fact.'

The certainty carried in her voice, as if there was no doubt. When, deep down, he doubted himself often. 'Thank you for your confidence. What else do you see?'

She smiled again, a beautiful thing which lit up the room better than the late-morning light.

'Fishing for compliments?'

'Wanting to know how well you know your subject.'

She brought her hand to her mouth. Tapped her lips with her index finger.

'You appear cold, aloof, but you're not. That's the Prince of Lasserno's costume, what you allow the world to see, but it's not real. You care, deeply, for your country and your people, but you refuse to show it to anyone. As if you're not the man, but you *are* the crown. Except there's a human heart beating in your chest. But some days, I think you wish there wasn't. Because being human is messy and ugly and imperfect.

It's about desire and need and feelings, and that's not who you want to be. The trouble is, that's exactly who you are.'

Each word hit him like an arrow shot straight, finding its truest and most damaging place. She saw him too well, and her insights caused his heart to race, his chest to constrict.

Others only saw what they assumed was the truth. He could control the narrative with them. Like acting, putting on a show. Right now, Hannah was all risk. Huge reward, but the risk terrified him most of all. She gave him the tantalising glimpse of a life without meticulous attention to duty, and that was a terrible temptation.

'I think that you're worried if you show people the real you, they won't love you. The thing is, they'd love you even more if you would be yourself. Because you're a good man.'

He didn't want to talk now, but he couldn't move. It was as though he was pinned to the bed, frozen in place. He couldn't take this attention on him. He didn't know why he had asked the question of her, because he should have known she'd see things he hadn't wanted others to see.

'Do you want to know what I see in you?' he asked, trying to deflect from himself because the spotlight burned too brightly when it focused on the truth.

'Not really.' She closed her notepad, sat up straighter. So perfect and relaxed in her nakedness.

'Why is that, Hannah?'

She hid herself as well. They both wore costumes, even now pretending to be something they weren't.

'I'm not that interesting.'

'I disagree. Rule number one, remember.'

She rolled her eyes. 'Yes, Your Highness.'

As he was a prince, people didn't mock or tease him. Or joke with him much at all. Stefano was the only person who did, but he'd been a friend for years. Alessio found himself enjoying it from her. The irreverence. The freedom for them both to...*be.*

'You talk about me hiding myself? You do it too. You're a passionate woman when it comes to your art. But you deny that part of yourself, forgetting what you're like in my arms. In bed.'

'And what about you?' Hannah said. 'Wanting to marry someone you barely know and don't love. Better not to marry at all.'

He didn't want to think of marriage, matchmakers, or perfect princesses right now, but they were the reality he couldn't escape. A shortlist of candidates was on his desk, whom he would meet…when Hannah left.

'I have a dynasty to preserve.'

'What if your precious yet-to-be-found princess falls in love with you and you don't love her? Where will you be then? You're condemning someone to a life that's unfair.'

'She'll know what to expect.'

'Or are you afraid of forming a real attachment? That's when you have most to lose.'

Her words hit sharp and true. He couldn't let them go unanswered. He sat up, the sheet falling from his torso. Hannah's cheeks pinked, but she didn't look away.

'Says the woman who claims she's not interested in love. That her art is enough.'

'At least I'm not trying to draw anyone else into it. This is my life. I'll live it how I see fit.'

She stood and sauntered to him, beautifully naked, the rolling sway of her hips and tight nipples, the slight flush on her chest were telling him what she had in mind. Distraction. And he didn't care because her kind of distraction was the most delicious of all. Let them both drown in it, forgetting everything else.

'You're so perfect in everything you do. Even now, lying in this bed. As if you're artfully displayed. It makes me wonder if you know how to be anything less. Makes me want to mess you up.'

'I invite you to try.'

There was something about her that warned of danger. Like an impending storm, dark and brooding, hovering on the horizon. The bed dipped as she sat on the edge close to him, her fingers blackened from the charcoal she'd smudged across her page. Hannah reached out with one hand to his chest and smeared her fingers across his flesh, leaving dark stripes there. The smile on her face was pure wickedness. 'How does that feel, Your Highness?'

'Like you're not trying hard enough.'

Her pupils flared as she rose to his challenge and climbed over him, straddling his body. Rocking on the hardness between his thighs. He sat forward to wrap his arms around her but she planted her hands flat on his chest and pushed. He fell back, enjoying her new assertion far too much. Hannah took his face in her hands, rubbed

her thumbs over his cheeks. He didn't need to
see in the mirror to know that she was marking
him with the charcoal on her fingers. As if she
were claiming ownership. His blood rang in a
furious roar as he enjoyed her possession, as if
with each stroke she were writing *mine* on his
skin. She leaned forward, her lips touching his.
Her mouth open, lush. Claiming him. He let her.
In this fantasy, for these few days they could be
anything they desired. He took what she gave,
his hands at her hips as she moved against him.
The sheet between them an interruption, a distraction, but necessary. How he wanted to slide
into her with no protection, forget they were the
Prince and his artist.

She broke the kiss and he almost thrust his
hands into her hair and dragged her to him once
more, but the way she leaned back with a subtle
smile on her lips suggested she was admiring
her handiwork.

'Condom,' she said, as she cupped his jaw and
traced her thumb almost lovingly in another
stripe along his cheek.

He didn't need to be asked twice, reaching
to the bedside table where he'd left a number
rather than fumble for a packet and interrupt

these fleeting moments. Hannah sat back as he grabbed a sliver of foil, tore it open.

'You're going to have to move,' he said. His hands trembled with the desire to be inside her. She shifted back as he shoved down the sheet and rolled the protection in place. All the while she watched him, her fascination with his body addictive, her attention on him complete.

She placed her hand on his chest again. 'Now lie back and relax.'

He almost laughed. How could he relax when he was wound so tight he wanted to snap? His thighs shook. The whole of him quivered with barely restrained desire. It was like nothing he had ever experienced. She positioned herself over him and lowered slowly. He watched her body take him, the shock of the feeling, coupled with the vision, electric. Her head thrown back, hair tumbling over her shoulders, nipples tight and beading with arousal. Such an erotic picture she painted for him. Hannah rode his body as he thrust up into her. Lost in her heat. The sounds she made. Her pure, erotic abandon had the tight, bright sting of arousal crack and shatter with one hard, sharp thrust and shout. Then Hannah tightened around him and broke as well, falling forward onto his heaving chest as he wrapped his arms round her.

'You're well messed-up now,' she said with a shaky laugh, which told him she was probably *well messed-up* herself. And there was nothing he could say or do because she was right. The problem was, he might never wish to go back to his tidy, perfect, righteous life, ever again.

CHAPTER TEN

TWO NIGHTS AND three days of bliss and it was now over.

Hannah sat in the front of an anonymous-looking grey car with Alessio at the wheel. They'd spent the early morning swimming in the deep, cobalt waters of the Mediterranean. Avoiding the inevitable. Pretending the world couldn't touch them. It touched them now. Everything tightening, tensing.

As they drove towards the outskirts of Lasserno's capital, where they would return to the palace, Alessio began to change the most. It was like watching the ground freeze over by degrees. As if the cold chill of winter were creeping up on them, slowly and relentlessly. Where once he'd been loose and relaxed, all of him seemed to be on high alert. Their easy conversation on the yacht dried away, his grip on the steering wheel almost white-knuckled.

She settled back and tried to relax into the seat.

The fantasy of the weekend was well and truly over, those few days where they ate, slept, made love, soon to be but a precious memory. She'd thought this would be enough, that she'd be un-affected by it all. But what she hadn't banked on was how much changed when you got to see a real person. And Alessio had become real to her. Not a prince like he was on paper but a mag-nificent, kind, self-deprecating man who could make her laugh and would soon make her cry, of that she had no doubt.

She wanted to cry for him now. She didn't know how he'd marry some princess in a cold, practical relationship, when their own days had been full to the brim with passion. She couldn't see him as surviving with anything less than what they had had. She could barely take in any air at those thoughts. Of Alessio married, with children. Without her. The idea of him in any other woman's arms thrust through her with all the brutality of a sword to the heart. She looked over at him. His jaw was set, as though he was steeling himself for a life he didn't want.

As if he knew she was looking at him, Alessio turned his head a fraction. 'You've had a touch of the sun. Your skin's pink.'

She shrugged, blinking away the burn in her eyes. His concern and notice could undo her, and she wasn't sure there was thread enough in the world to stitch herself together again. 'I'll be fine. It's a little sunburn.'

'I should have paid more attention.' She couldn't see his eyes, hidden behind sunglasses as they were, but his voice was filled with care. 'Remembered the sunscreen. Your beautiful skin is so pale.'

'Too much time indoors, painting.' She'd never felt like that before, but there'd been a blissful sense of freedom to being in the sunshine, the breeze in her hair. Something other than standing in her studio surrounded by solvent and paints. The same way she'd forgotten the joy of being on horseback, not practising her showjumping, just the pleasure of the ride. All the small things she'd shoved away from herself over the years. Perhaps when she returned home, she could buy a little horse. Take some time to ride again. If she could afford to, because even with Alessio's commission, funds would still be tight. But there was a kernel of hope there, for something more, even if she couldn't have him.

Hannah let out a slow, even breath. She'd not

be here much longer and time seemed to be speeding up and careening away.

'I'd like to do a bit of sightseeing in the capital before I leave. I should get a souvenir for Sue.'

She had many things to thank her agent for. Many things to curse her for as well, with this commission. It had shown her life had possibilities again, whilst also snatching them away.

'I'll arrange security for you. A list of places to go.'

It sounded as if he was making himself responsible for her, and that was something she didn't need when they should be pulling apart rather than meshing even further.

'I hardly think I'll have a problem buying a snow globe or something similar. Who'd be interested in me?'

His hands flexed on the steering wheel, though his focus remained resolutely on the road ahead.

'I want you to be safe. I want that for you.'

The words were loaded because she was sure he meant far more. Hannah squashed down the lick of heat running through her. He was a good man. He cared. The way he did with the children at the hospital, that was all. It meant nothing more.

It couldn't.

He was not safe, not for her. Not ever. With him, she found herself wanting things she'd not contemplated for years, and those things could crack her in two. Because love meant leaving the door open to your own destruction and inviting the destroyer in. She could never give her whole heart because then she'd lose all over again, and she wasn't sure she'd survive it when she barely had last time.

'I'd like to go on my own. Having security would be strange and take the fun away from things. But I'll take a list of places to go. Thank you.'

'If I could have come with—'

'You're the Prince of Lasserno.' She put him back in that box where he should remain. Would even tie it with a tight, bright gold ribbon to keep him firmly back in place. 'You can't just go sightseeing with some random tourist.'

'You're not a random tourist, Hannah.' His voice was soft. The cabin of the car filled with the weight of things unsaid. Of how much more this, between them, had become.

'I'm sure you'll have too much to do.'

Alessio checked his watch, now firmly back on

his wrist as if it had never left. 'Always. I may have a parliament for advice, but in the end, this is an absolute monarchy. There is only me.'

There is only me.

He'd never let anyone in, and it struck her as sad and exhausting.

The roads were busier as they approached the capital but the run to the palace seemed clear. As she sat staring at the castle looming on the horizon the roar of a motorcycle came from behind, louder, closing in. Then it was right there. At the passenger side. Two people, one driving, one pillion. Something in their hand. Camera. Trying to shove it against the window of the car. A flash.

She reflexively held up her hand against the tinted glass, her heart pounding a sickening tempo. Another flash. Alessio hissed something through his teeth. She didn't need to understand Italian to know he swore. He grabbed the brim of his cap and pulled it lower. Hannah wore nothing on her head but did have sunglasses. She pushed them up her nose, not that it would make much difference.

'In the glove compartment there's a cap. Put it on. Pull the sun visor down.'

She did as he said. The motorcycle sped ahead while the passenger turned, trying to get photos through the windscreen. A shrill tone rang out through the car. Alessio's phone. He answered hands-free and a terse voice filled the interior, speaking rapid Italian. Stefano.

She couldn't understand what they said, but the fury in Alessio's voice, the tight, cold rage, chilled the car by degrees. She wrapped her arms round herself as she took in the importance of what was happening. But what did the press know? It could be he'd taken her out sightseeing as he'd suggested, the Prince showing a guest around his country. That was easily enough explained, wasn't it?

The call disconnected. Silence filled the car apart from Alessio's hard, jagged breaths.

'I'm sorry,' she said, because what more was there to say? 'It might not be that bad.'

'It is *that bad*.' His grip tightened on the wheel again, his mouth a thin, hard line. 'They are at the palace. Every entrance, though the western gate apparently has fewer.'

'Can we—?'

'Not now.' He took one hand from the tight grip of the wheel and dragged it over his face.

She'd been royally dismissed. Experienced it in the sharp cut of his voice. In the way all of the warmth had left him, and he'd turned into Lasserno's ruler once more. Another motorcycle joined the first. Alessio kept the speed steady and didn't try to outrun them, for which she was thankful. She stopped looking at the road in front and instead stared down at her lap, her fingers twisting in the soft fabric of her dress. Maybe no one would know who she was, but a sick feeling of bile rose in her throat. Her quiet, anonymous life in the country was likely to be shattered. The protection of those walls she'd built around herself—her art, her peace—all crumbling away. The palace loomed large ahead, and she saw it now like a kind of prison. They didn't approach from the front, or from the entrance they'd sneaked out of only three blissful days earlier, but a side entrance where palace guards stood, holding back a throng of photographers jostling for position. If this was the western gate, she'd hate to see what the others were like.

The car pushed through into a large courtyard. Alessio stopped, switched off the engine. Sat for a few moments then turned to her. She couldn't see his eyes behind the sunglasses but the whole atmosphere inside the car felt accusatory. As if somehow, she was to blame for this. Then he opened the door, thrusting it wide as he launched himself from the car and slammed it shut behind him.

Hannah took off her cap to put it back in the glove compartment and grabbed her handbag before following, running to keep up as Alessio barely broke his stride, his staff bowing as he passed, looking at her with some curiosity.

She didn't know how long they walked through what appeared to be service corridors, until they reached a vast, familiar hall and a door she immediately recognised. Alessio's office. Inside, Stefano stood by one of the mullioned windows, speaking rapid-fire on the phone. When they entered, he hung up. Alessio tore off his sunglasses and cap, tossed them on his desk. He and Stefano exchanged a look—Stefano's all sympathy, Alessio's barely concealed fury.

'What's being said?'

'They know about the hospital visits. That's been online already.'

'The families?'

'Are being protected. They won't talk. You know that.'

Alessio's head dropped. He stared at the carpet as if a solution could be divined there. All the while, Hannah realised she was superfluous. And she didn't know what to do. Stand. Sit. Pace. Everyone in this room was still. Her, Alessio, Stefano. Like chess pieces waiting for the first move.

'They're using the sick children to make a story about me.'

'It's not a bad thing, since it's a good story. As I've said before.'

'What about this?' Alessio waved his hands between him and Hannah, as if she were nothing. His dismissal sliced sharp and fresh like a paper cut.

Stefano deigned to look at her then. Nice to know she existed. She couldn't tell what he was thinking, everything about him inscrutable in those moments. But he seemed paler, his eyes tight. No tie, the top button of his shirt undone.

'The speculation online is intense, but only in the less reputable media...for now. The photographs of you in the car will break soon enough. Who knows what they'll say? My staff won't talk, if that's your concern.'

'They never have before. I have *no* concerns there.'

'I have a team considering the problem.' Stefano looked at her again and in the deep pit of her stomach she knew *she* was the problem here. Something to be dealt with. Not a person with fears of her own. 'I'll see them now, on how we manage things going forward.'

He left the room and Alessio walked to the window, looked out over Lasserno. His country. The only thing he desired or needed, she was coming to realise.

'Never complain, never explain,' she said.

He wheeled round, all of him so hard and tense it was as if one more push and he might snap. She wanted to do something. Reach out. Comfort. Say it would all be okay. But she knew some things would never be okay again, for either of them.

'What?'

'The British Royal family. That's what they do.'

'Trust me.' He began to pace the room in that familiar way of his, as if he needed to expend energy. 'I won't be giving statements.'

'How did the press find out?'

He raised one coal-dark eyebrow at her, the burnt umber gaze of his so heated only hours ago, now cold and forbidding like some bottomless, muddy pool. 'How, indeed?'

'You think...me?'

He looked so out of place in this moment, in his disarray. Wearing casual clothes and not the suit he donned as his usual armour. Surrounded by his ancestors glaring down from their lofty height on the walls, as if the weekend of humanity he'd stolen was some kind of disgrace.

'I trust everyone else around me. But this story is a familiar one.'

It dawned on her then, what he wouldn't say out loud. He didn't trust *her*. 'It might be an annoyance for your private life, but have you ever thought how this debacle could affect me?'

He stopped his pacing. Dead.

'You?'

Said as if he'd only just realised she was a person who might have thoughts and feelings about this too. She threw up her hands and began pacing then. As if Alessio's will to constantly be on the move had infected her.

'No, clearly you haven't thought about me at all. Other than to accuse me.'

'I've accused you of nothing.'

The *yet* hung unsaid.

'I sign non-disclosure agreements with all of my clients. My word about what I discover is absolute. Would any of them trust me if they thought I would spill my secrets to the press? No. Sure, I could paint people, but it would never be the same. It would destroy my process. Ruin *everything.*'

The corner of his mouth rose in something like a sneer. Not quite contempt, but close enough.

'You're financially distressed. Your uncle mismanaged your inheritance. A tell-all about me would fill your bank account,' Alessio hissed, cold, cruel and furious.

She stopped then, as if those words had stripped the will to move right out of her. There was such accusation in his gaze. It was as though he was a brittle shell filled with nothing but disdain.

'You honestly believe I would talk about this, us...' she waved between them as he had done, only this had meant something to her '...to the press? What kind of world do you live in?'

'Look around you.' He spread his arms wide, like some sacrifice. 'I live in the real world!

Where people want what they can't have and take what they can.'

His words cracked her, cleaving her in two. She grabbed on to the back of an armchair and gripped the silken fabric tight in case the halves of her fell to the floor. 'If this is the real world then I don't want any part of it.'

'Luckily for you, you shall have none.'

A reminder once again she was being firmly put in her place. A place she'd never sought to leave, until the weekend just past. 'I know.'

'Do you? I'm glad to hear it, since you'll leave today. Within the hour. I'll have your things sent to you. My jet—'

She shook her head. Let go of the armchair's support. She needed none. She'd lived on her own terms almost since the day her parents had died. She'd do it again. As for now, she needed to get away from him, from his life and the trappings of it. Get back to the comfort and safety of her home and her relative anonymity. She didn't want sorrowful looks from royal flight attendants as she wept into a cup of tea.

Because she'd cry, but not in front of him.

'I'll fly on some airline.'

He shook his head. 'You think the press in

Lasserno are bad? They're kittens compared to what you're walking into. How will you drive home, on narrow country roads being chased by motorcycles? Cars? I think not.'

If he were concerned he might have looked stricken, but that wasn't what was happening here. He didn't care about her. He never really had. His reputation was his only interest and everything else was peripheral. But there was one thing they needed to address: what she was being paid to do, since she was just an employee now.

'Your portrait.'

Something about him changed then. Alessio seemed to straighten, stand taller. Even if you didn't know it, seeing him in this moment you'd realise he was ruler of all he surveyed. Uncompromising and absolute.

'I want no portrait. Every time anyone looks at the painting, they'll speculate about what *you* saw and exactly how much. It can *never* be what I wanted it to be, a statement of intent. I'll find someone else. But don't fear. You'll be paid for your time.'

There was the final blow, his words like a kick to the stomach. It was as if for a second time her world had been taken from her. All of this, here, had been for nothing.

If she weren't made of stronger stuff, she might bend in two. But she'd survived the death of her parents and her horse, the rejection of her boyfriend, the dishonesty of her uncle. She could survive Alessio Arcuri. And she'd show him.

'You'll pay me…for my *time*. My…services rendered. What a fine way to make a woman feel cheap.' She took a deep breath, looked him straight in the eye so he could see how strong she really was, and just how much he'd meant to her until this. 'I don't want to be paid. I want nothing from you. So go and find your perfect princess. I hear royal weddings and babies are big news. They'll erase any rumours about me from your life.'

She turned her back on him, needing to get out and get away. Wanting to run but carrying herself with all the dignity she deserved, because she wasn't at fault, even though this whole place seemed intent on blaming her. Instead, she injected steel into her spine and walked to the door with her head held high. Walked away from him. As she reached out for the door handle, she hesitated. Not turning, because she didn't want to see Alessio ever again. Seeing him might remind her of what she'd lost. What she never really had in the first place.

'Thank you, Your Highness, for making our parting so much easier.'

CHAPTER ELEVEN

ALESSIO STARED AT the broken-apart travelling crate. The wood was scattered about the floor of his office after he'd cracked it apart with the crowbar he'd asked his staff to deliver here. That infernal wooden case had taunted him from the moment it had been delivered a few days before. No note, no explanation. A return address for Ms Hannah Barrington the only suggestion of what it contained.

A portrait. One he didn't want, but one he got anyway.

And *this* portrait. He stood back. This wasn't a painting to be hung in a throne room. It was deeply, achingly personal and he had no idea what to do with it. Because as he looked at the picture, what he saw was not the man he stared at in the mirror every morning but another self. Real. A better version of him.

There was no elegant quality to the brush-strokes. They slashed across the canvas with a terrifying brutality. *He* was the sole focus of the artist's gaze. Sitting side-on, with his head turned to the painter. White shirt slightly unkempt, open at the neck. Hair unruly as if he'd rolled out of bed and raked his hands through it, sat in a chair and looked at the person holding the brush. Hannah. His fingers were steepled, contemplating her. Eyes intense and focused, fixed on one woman, as if he would never look away. Corners of his lips tilted in the merest of smiles in a moment where it seemed some secret had been told, which only the painter and the subject knew.

This was a picture for a private space, for a bedroom, where the intimacies it spoke of could be understood only by the people who saw it each day.

From the packing had also fallen two small spiral sketchbooks, those she'd carried around with her. He flicked through them. There was the small landscape in watercolour pencil she'd done when she'd first arrived. The view from her window. The rest were sketches of him. His hands, his eyes. Lips. Rough outlines of him stalking the floor. Smiling. Naked in bed on Stefano's yacht. His life, the man, in black, white and grey.

In the beginning, he recognised the person in those pictures. Cold, aloof. Remote from everything around him. As they progressed, Hannah had seen him in ways he no longer saw himself, seen the tiny glimpses of happiness. And then those when they were together, alone. In them, he was unrecognisable.

A man changed.

He glanced at the desk, where a folder lay: his shortlist of princesses. They were everything he'd asked for. Bright, beautiful, intelligent women from royalty who understood the job they'd be asked to do. He'd been to dinner with a few and each time he had, every part of him rebelled. Spending even a second with a woman who was not Hannah felt like a betrayal.

Because no matter how he'd tried to forget her, he couldn't. Work didn't help. Riding Apollo didn't help. Nothing did. Her touch, her laugh, the scent of her like autumn apples…all embedded in his memory. And now he had the portrait, which hinted at something he dared not name because of what he'd done to her.

He loathed how she'd looked at him on her last day here. As if he'd warped something perfect, to make it ugly. Taking his fears and frustrations out on her, when she was the victim. Because she wasn't the perpetrator, of that he was sure. He had all the power. She was the one with everything to lose. A rumoured affair with his artist had risen as a moment of brief interest in a world of many such events and faded away. All the while she'd maintained a dignified silence. His father might have laughed at the evidence of his son's human failings, though to Alessio those taunts were now meaningless. All he'd been obsessed by was its effect on her, trawling her name in the daily international press, but she was a secondary character in a story already forgotten by everyone except him.

The door of his palace office opened, and Stefano walked in. Hesitated beside the picture still half in its packing case. Nudged the crowbar discarded on the carpet beside it with the toe of his shoe.

'I thought you'd send it back or put it away without looking at it.'

He'd wanted to. The sheer terror of what Hannah might have painted had stopped him breaking open the picture for days. But he'd needed to exorcise her, and he thought, by finally confronting the portrait, that he would. He hadn't, and in fact it had made things worse.

'It's only a painting.' The lie stuck in his throat. It was more than that. So much more. A mirror to possibilities he'd rejected in a way that couldn't easily be repaired.

'If you say so.'

His friend looked drawn and tired. As if he carried a burden too heavy for one man. No enthusiasm left in him. Stefano hadn't been the same since Hannah had left the palace. Alessio thought it was managing the press fallout, the work since. He began to realise how much he missed, and how this might be something more.

'What do you say?' Alessio asked.

'I say we've both made terrible mistakes, and now it's time to face them.'

Something about the weight of those words carried a warning that things might never be the same again. 'I don't know what you mean.'

'You're not a stupid man, my friend. I don't need to point out your grave error. As for mine...' Stefano handed Alessio an envelope. 'My resignation.'

A terrible cold settled over Alessio, even in the middle of Lasserno's glorious summer. As if everything were changing and he would be the ultimate loser. Stefano stood back. Formal. Aloof. An employee and nothing more. Alessio wouldn't accept it. Right now, things needed to stay the same.

'No. Whatever the problem is, I'll fix it. Do you need a holiday? A pay rise?'

Stefano laughed. There was no humour in the tone. It sounded like a mockery of all things happy. 'Ever the Prince. There are some things you can't repair with money or power.'

'Why are you doing this?'

Stefano didn't answer. He turned, walked towards Hannah's painting. Alessio wanted to hide it. Keep it to himself. Such a deeply private piece left him vulnerable, as though everything about him was set to be exposed, his darkest hopes and dreams, which only Hannah knew.

'She's in love with you,' Stefano said.

'What?' A bright burst of something perfect, like hope, tore through him. A cruel sensation when he had nothing to hope for after what he'd done.

'As I said, you're not a stupid man. *Look* at the picture.' Stefano pointed at it, his finger stabbing the air. 'What you need in your life, Alessio, is someone to see you like *that*. The man behind the mask of the prince. You also need someone in your life you can look at as you looked at Hannah in that very moment.'

Inside he *knew*. This was a picture painted by someone who saw the soul of another person. That didn't come simply by fine observation. It was more. Hannah had quietly given him her heart somewhere in the two weeks they'd been together. He'd selfishly taken it, and cruelly rejected it when she'd asked for nothing in return but his respect.

The problem was, he'd given her his heart as well, which was why everything seemed broken. Because she'd taken it back to England when she'd gone, and now he was left only half a man.

'Is *this* why you're resigning?'

Stefano slowly shook his head, as if the movement was too wearying to bear.

'I'm resigning because, whilst you *might* be able to repair your great error, I can't repair mine. You want to know who leaked to the press? I did.'

Alessio dropped into the chair behind his desk. He had no power to move, like a child's toy whose batteries had gone dead.

'You threw Hannah and me to those leeches?' A wicked fire lit inside, the burn threatening to overwhelm him. He clenched his fists. If he hadn't known Stefano his whole life he might have thrown punches in this moment. But there was so much he'd missed with Hannah, what hadn't he seen with his oldest friend?

Stefano shoved his hands in the pockets of his trousers. Dropped his head. 'Only about your visit to the hospital. What I failed to recognise is that small piece of information would start press interest about what else you might be doing in secret. *That's* what led to them discovering about you and Hannah. And I'll never forgive myself for it.'

It was as if the floor fell out beneath him. Alessio gripped the arms of his chair to hold himself stable when nothing in his life was any more.

'*Dio!* Stefano. Why?'

'You hide all of yourself. What you present to the world is a version of who you think everyone should see. Yet that image didn't comfort the people of Lasserno. It made them fear they were getting someone who didn't care for them at all, and that opinion was bleeding into the press. I thought a small glimpse of the private man would help show people who you truly are. And that it would allow you to see past the constraints you impose upon yourself, to the *possibilities*. Instead I caused greater harm.'

Alessio nodded. What more could he do? He'd lost everything. Hannah. His best friend. He couldn't fathom Stefano's betrayal. He couldn't forgive himself for what he'd done to Hannah, driven by fear of finding something real.

'You need a person you can trust in this position. I've arranged for someone temporary to take my place. There were a few good candidates in the palace.'

'That's…acceptable.' Alessio didn't know what more to say. His world crumbled around him with Stefano the last brick to fall.

His friend walked towards the door of the office for the last time. Just as Hannah had walked away only months before.

'My family has served yours for centuries. But you must believe this has never been work for me. It's been my pleasure as your friend.'

He then stopped…hesitated with his hand still resting on the doorknob.

'I have some advice. From Machiavelli. *"Any man who tries to be good all the time is bound to come to ruin among the great number who are not good."* Allow yourself some imperfections. You have a chance to make things right. I've run out of mine.'

Stefano gave a final bow and shut the door. And for the first time in his life Alessio felt completely alone.

Hannah stood in her studio, the window opening wide onto the sunny garden beyond. This place had once been her oasis of peace, where she could lose herself. Now it seemed more like a prison. She flopped into the threadbare sofa in a dusty corner, cup of tea in hand, body sluggish with a tiredness that hadn't seemed to have left her since she'd returned home. Self-inflicted to be sure, but it was as though she'd never feel awake again, this pressing lassitude which had stolen over her.

From the moment she'd walked into this space on returning from Lasserno she'd begun to work, grabbing a canvas and painting with a ferocity which shut everything out. She'd worked all day and through the nights. Barely sleeping or eating till she'd finished Alessio's portrait. Pouring all her heart and most of her soul into the picture to get one man out of her life. The tears and the pain worked through her fingers onto the canvas, then she'd let it go.

Or that was what was supposed to have happened. In the past, each time she'd finished a portrait had been like a great cleansing. She'd send the picture on its way and leave its subject behind as a fond memory whilst she started afresh.

Not this time. The ache of loss remained like a wound unhealed, as if the bleeding out would never stop. Hannah realised what it was now. All that time she'd spent shielding herself from the pain of love and her heart had gone and fallen in love anyway. At least she'd learned something. Suffering this kind of pain wouldn't break her. Even though the colours of the world didn't seem right, as if everything were sepia-toned, she was still standing. One day she might even be able to look back to a time when for a few fantasy moments she was made to believe she could be a princess.

She hadn't been treated like a princess in the end, though. That Alessio believed she might betray what they'd shared had shredded what remained of her heart. It told Hannah that, whilst what had happened was of great moment to her, to Alessio it meant nothing. It can't have, or he would never have thought she'd talk to the press.

Sure, they'd sniffed around when she returned to the UK, offering large sums for an exclusive. It would have solved all her financial woes, just as he'd accused. But the idea of betraying those precious moments with Alessio made her sick to the stomach.

And yet, some money had arrived in her account. Whilst she'd refused it back in Lasserno, Sue had been more circumspect when contacted by the palace. Now there were funds enough to keep the sharks at bay. It might not refill the coffers her uncle had raided, but it would do. Her uncle's assets were being sold to help pay his debts, and that would help too. She could rebuild. She had her art. Things would be fine. Truly fine.

If only she could plug the Alessio-sized hole in her heart.

She stared at the blank canvas on her easel, one she had no inspiration for. At least, not for the intended subject. Another consumed all her interest. A man with black hair and umber eyes and a glance which could set her aflame. If she picked up a pencil now she'd be able to perfectly reproduce the crinkles at the corners of his eyes when he smiled, the sensual curve of his lips when he looked at her. It was as if she would always be able to draw him. He was embedded inside her. Yet a prince had no part in her life. She went to the window. Breathed the warm air. Tried reminding herself that these simple things were what made her happy. One day her heart *would* believe her head, but not today.

The tinkle of the doorbell woke Hannah from her inertia. She'd had a few visitors since she'd returned here. Kind people in the village bringing jams, biscuits and sympathy. Probably seeking gossip, but she gave them none and the small tokens had helped.

She made her way to the front door. Pulled a band from the pocket of her jeans and raked her hair into an untidy knot on her head. Steeled herself for a visitor she didn't really want. She'd had a spyhole installed at the suggestion of the local constable when some of the press had become more insistent. Out of caution she peeked through.

Alessio.

She grabbed on to the door jamb to hold herself upright, her heart rate spiking at the thrill of seeing him again, even through the dim fisheye glass. She'd tried telling herself over and over he didn't matter but her heart now called her out as a liar. Hannah froze. Open the door? Ignore it? Tell him to go away? She stood back, trying to steady her rapid breathing, and jumped when the bell gave another short, sharp burst. In that moment she acted on impulse, turning the key and wrenching at the door.

He came into view in a dizzying rush, like the swoop of a roller coaster. More beautiful than she remembered, but then Alessio had always seemed hyper-real to her. He wore an immaculate blue suit, pristine white shirt, bold viridian tie. Nothing at all conciliatory about him, clothed in his armour of choice, as if ready for battle. The only thing about him that wasn't perfect was the stubble on his jaw of a day or two unshaven. The contrast between that casual aberration and the rest of him made her treacherous little heart flutter like the butterflies around the hollyhocks in her garden.

'Hannah.'

The way he said her name… It tumbled from his lips as if the syllables hurt to speak them. As if it had so much meaning. She wanted to mean something to him, but it was a fool's game she had no time to play. She knew her place, and needed to remind herself of it, so she dropped herself into a deep curtsey. 'Your Highness.'

He winced. 'There's no need. Not after—'

'Of course there's a need. What did your dossier say? *"The first time you meet His Royal Highness in the day, you shall curtsey."*'

'We're not in the palace.'

'No, we're definitely not.' She gripped the door, focused on the cut of the wood into her palm. Better that than focusing on the pain in what remained of her heart. 'Did you come looking for more horses? Because there are none here.'

'I'm looking for something, but not horses.'

'And no private secretary to act as a shield between you and me. What a risk-taker you are. How people might talk.'

He dropped his head, looking at the doorstep. To the worn doormat, the faded "Welcome" she'd meant to replace but never seemed to find the time.

'Any risk to me here is deserved. May I come inside?'

She didn't want him here and craved him all

the same, the emotions confused and jumbled in a way she couldn't sort out. Curdling in her stomach like an ill-chosen meal.

'What are you doing here?'

'I need to…talk.'

'I'm not sure I need to listen.'

He shoved his hands in the pockets of his trousers. 'I deserve that. But I'd still like you to hear what I have to say. Please.'

She studied him now, in a way she hadn't allowed herself only moments before. Part curiosity, part need. Those lines around his eyes that creased when he smiled appeared more pronounced, though the look wasn't a happy one. There were dark smudges underneath his eyes as if she'd run her charcoal-covered fingers there. That thought was a reminder of a blissful afternoon on Stefano's yacht when everything had seemed so perfect. But she shouldn't reminisce about those few days—they were long gone. Still, listening didn't cost her much and might give them both some closure, far enough away from their tortured last day. She stepped back and allowed him in. He crowded out the small entry foyer.

'Come to the studio.'

That was her war room, where she usually felt competent and safe. Though everything seemed a risk to her right now. Once again, Alessio was her greatest danger, and yet she still wanted to poke her fingers into the fire and be burned. But she'd remind them both of her place in his life.

'I should thank you for the payment, even though you went against my wishes.'

'I took two weeks of your time. It was the least I could do.'

The least he could do... The pain of that morning roared back in a rush and she couldn't hold it in. She didn't care any more, striding right up to him, invading his space. Wanting to push him away and hold on tight, all at the same time. The burn of tears pricked at her eyes, but she was *done* crying. Too many tears had been shed over him already.

She planted her hands on her hips. Better than reaching out to touch.

'I would have walked away, at the end of it all. After those two weeks, I would have stepped onto a plane and you would never have heard from me again.' As much as her heart had rebelled at the time, it was what she would have done because he was looking for someone other than her. Because she loved him and that was what you were supposed to do when you loved something: you set it free. 'But you cheapened *everything*. Turned something beautiful into something dirty.'

'I know. Only one of us was acting like an adult that day. I hurt you intentionally.'

She bit on her lower lip, hoping the sting might take her mind off the pain his admission caused.

'Is that what this is, a kind of sorry? You didn't need to fly all the way here. You could have sent a card. *My deepest apologies for being a jerk.* Maybe some flowers as a final kind of blow-off.'

Alessio stood there. Immaculate. Impassive. Taking what she gave. Even though he appeared a little careworn, it only added to his underlying appeal.

'I'll never forgive myself for how I treated you. I was afraid of what I felt but the coward in me chose to believe I meant no more to you than the money I could provide. That's *my* issue. I shouldn't have cheapened the most treasured time of my life because of fear, when the perpetrator of the press leak was closer to home.'

'Who talked?' Alessio trusted everyone in the palace. He had assured her that what they had could be kept secret. And yet someone had betrayed him. It had to hurt for a man like Alessio, that misplaced confidence. She saw the cracks in his façade then, not only the two-day growth and tired eyes, but also his slightly paler skin. The tightness around his mouth. All of him looking older and more deeply etched than before.

'Stefano.'

It was as if a rock had settled in the pit of her stomach. She almost reached out to him, to comfort. But Alessio hadn't wanted her before, and if he pushed her away again she might never recover. There were some memories she wouldn't allow to become any more tainted.

'I'm sorry.' She meant it. She understood betrayal from someone she should have been able to trust too. 'Did he say why?'

Alessio might have been cruel to her but she wouldn't be the same to him. She was better than that. He walked over to the battered table holding her paint, brushes and palette.

'His intentions were good, but misplaced. And yet I can't find it in my heart to blame him.' He mindlessly sorted through the tubes of paint. Picked one up. 'Alizarin Crimson. The colour of righteous anger.'

He might have smiled then. Something about him seemed to lighten for a moment, the hint of his lips turning up at the corners. It softened him, like a dry brush smudging over the sharp edges of a painted line.

'You remembered,' she said. A door inside her that should have been locked tight opened a fraction. But they wanted different things, didn't they? He'd told her from the beginning. Yet her silly heart simply craved to beat to a singular rhythm.

Alessio's.

'I remember everything. I can't forget. But I'm not good at the words for this.' He took off his coat, tossed it on the worn couch. Loosened his tie, as if he was going into a battle of another kind. An emotional one. 'I don't know how to be anything other than the Prince of Lasserno. It's all I was trained for. Then I received the portrait and drawings. And I finally saw myself through your eyes. I want to be *that* man. The one in the picture. I want to be that man, for you.'

Everything stopped. The silence, as if the universe waited and yet she couldn't quite fathom the words.

'What are you saying?'

'Do I have a chance to make this right?'

All colour in the world flooded back in a rush, as though things were too bright, too real. But the threat of his words crept up like some choking vine round her throat. That this couldn't work, that dreams didn't come true. Yet when she looked at him, all she saw on his face was hope. And her choice became clear. Saying no meant fear had won. Hannah was tired of losing that battle. She'd been afraid for long enough. It meant there was only one answer to give. So she let that hope fill her and overflow as she prepared to say one simple word.

'Yes.'

Yes. That single syllable went off like a bomb in Alessio's head, shattering everything. A chance. A fragile chance to repair what he'd broken. Build anew. She stood before him like a warrior. Tall. Proud. Putting him to shame. In her worn jeans with rips at the knees that perhaps hung a bit more loosely than the last time he'd seen her in them. Her hair in a messy topknot, strands falling about her face. Her green eyes flashing bright and vibrant, a warning to him that nothing here was certain. And yet he knew today was about laying his soul bare for her to trample on as she saw fit, even if it meant he lost the precious chance she'd granted him. Now was the time to be brave. As brave as her.

'I love you, Hannah.' Those words ground out of him, though easier than expected because they were his deepest truth. The root of all things good in his life. Her eyes widened a fraction, her hands clenched. He didn't know what those things meant, but he carried on regardless. She deserved these words; she should have nothing less. 'From the moment I saw you here I knew you were a danger to me, so to ruin any chance with you I was unspeakably cruel. But that doesn't change the *real* truth. There is only you.'

Her eyes gleamed a little brighter. Tears? What he wouldn't give to hold her, to tell her it would all be okay, but he couldn't, because he was the cause of her suffering.

'What about your perfect princess?'

'I've spent too long setting standards of perfection that were impossible for me to meet. I don't want some perfect princess. I need the woman who captured my heart.'

She turned and walked to the window, staring

outside into the rambling cottage garden, bright and beautiful in the English summer. Her hand reached up to her face, swiping at it.

'You hurt me. Claiming you now love me isn't a free pass.' Her voice was almost a whisper. The ache in it clawed at him, his own pain at what he'd done to her well deserved. His cross to bear. Alessio walked towards her, close enough to comfort if she eventually accepted it, far enough to give her the space she obviously needed.

'I know. All I've ever seen of love is that it brings pain. It seemed to be a poisoned thing. What I failed to realise is the great joy it can bring as well. I want to repair what I've done here, even if you can't love me back.'

Her shoulders hunched. She wrapped her arms round herself, as if she were trying to hold all the pain in. He hated that he'd done this. Failed the person he cared for the most.

'The problem is I can't *stop* loving you.'

He shut his eyes, giving a quiet thank-you to the heavens. It was as if everything that had been knotted up tight began to loosen. She loved him. She *still* loved him. His responsibility now was even greater than before. To honour her the way he should have from the beginning.

'I want to take the pain away by loving you back. Fiercely and for ever.'

Hannah turned, her eyes pink-rimmed. It was all he could do not to reach out and hold her, but he didn't have permission for that, not yet. She held out her hands in front of her, looked down at them. Splayed her fingers. The light from the window behind bathed her in an ethereal glow. She looked like a beautifully flawed angel.

'I'm pretty sure princesses don't have paint-stained hands.'

He feared he'd been the one to make her unsure about this, about herself, when he'd witnessed her being more regal than most royalty he'd ever met. Being a mere princess was beneath her. If he could make her a queen, he would.

'A princess can have whatever she wants. What *I* want is the artist who painted the portrait of the man now hanging in my bedroom. The man I should have aspired to be all these years. Not a prince, but a man in love. That love is what makes me a better person. There is no one other than you, Hannah. There never will be. The question is whether you want me for ever in return. And I'm prepared to wait. However long it takes.'

She looked up at him, eyes wide and sad and yet still tinged with hope, because it was all either of them had left. Hope that each would take a chance on the other, to build something towering and great, that could withstand anything life threw at them.

'What if however long is right now?'

He couldn't help the smile that broke out on his face, the fire of blazing happiness that lit inside. That she wanted him, that he was enough. The weight of the world rose from his shoulders. A lightening in his soul.

'Then I'll immediately accept whatever you allow. I don't expect your trust, perhaps not for years. But I'll fight for it each day. For you to be by my side. As my wife, my princess, my artist, my *everything*. You already own all my heart. Let me give you my whole world.'

She took a step towards him. 'You have my trust now. I'm not risking my heart for just anyone.'

Alessio opened his arms and Hannah walked right into them. He tightened them round her, soaking in her warmth, relishing in the feel of her body against his. His love. His heart. His home. She tilted her head up, her lips parted. He dropped his mouth to hers, the kiss coaxing, loving, saying in his gentle way what he had trouble verbalising. That he loved her more than words could ever express.

'It's no risk, *bella*.' That was his vow and promise, from this moment forward. 'I will cherish and care for your precious heart for ever.'

EPILOGUE

ALESSIO STROLLED THROUGH the doorway of the pavilion where Hannah now had her studio. The afternoon sun filtered like a patchwork through the windows, warming the space. She didn't look up at him as he entered. He loved that about her...her absolute focus when absorbed by her art.

No words were necessary to describe the love they shared, even in those moments. As she'd begun painting his coronation portrait he'd sat for her, stretches of blissful silence where he could watch her work. The concentration. She had it now, a tiny frown plaguing her forehead, as if something about the canvas troubled her. Something about him, since she was still working on his picture.

'I worry about you down here—it's too far from the palace.'

Her frown melted away. She looked up at him and smiled. The joy in it, seeing him, could light up his darkest places. When fear threatened, that he wouldn't be enough to guide the country through what was ahead of it, she could chase it away with the tilt of her perfect lips. With Hannah, there was no room for anything other than courage, love and trust.

'Don't be ridiculous. It's only a short stroll and the light's perfect.' She rose from the stool on which she'd been sitting and placed her hands on the small of her back, arching in a stretch. The soft fabric of her dress moulded to show off her rounded belly. Four months along and the pregnancy news in his country had reached fever pitch, with speculation over whether the baby would be a boy or a girl and bets being taken. Not even he and Hannah knew. Not yet. They wanted to keep some surprises, and to them it didn't matter. Either a little prince or princess would fill them with even more happiness, if that were possible.

He welcomed every moment of the bliss Hannah had brought to his life. A flood of warmth coursed over him. Love, pride. A whole mix that filled every day. He walked towards her, slowly, because she'd banned him from seeing his portrait until she was satisfied with it. He wondered if she ever would be.

'May I look now?' he asked.

'I think it's done.' That little frown was back again. He wanted to wipe it away, but at least the only time she ever seemed uncertain now was with her art. Not about his love, or her role. Never those things. He adored her; his people adored her. The murals she had designed and helped paint at the children's hospital had cemented Lasserno's love for its new Princess.

Even his father had given public praise for Alessio's choice of bride. Not that Alessio cared, but Hannah and her pregnancy had opened a door to communication that months ago would have seemed insurmountable. Perhaps miracles could happen. Alessio hadn't put any faith in them till Hannah's presence in his life made him believe anything was possible, including a truce with his father.

'What are you waiting for?' Hannah asked. Alessio shook himself out of his introspection. He walked round the canvas on the easel in the middle of the room and saw himself. It was like looking in a mirror. In this picture he sat in his office, surrounded by his ancestors. A magnificent representation of the Prince he'd once striven to be. His honours and regalia pinned to his military jacket. He didn't care for any of it.

The only honours he craved now were Hannah's.

'He seems almost forbidding. Unlike your other portrait.'

Strange how his perceptions of what his country needed from him had changed with Hannah's presence in his life, all the hard edges of himself burnished smooth by the love she brought to him. Love he wasn't afraid of any more. Her love made him strong, not weak.

'The first portrait is of the private man. The one only I'm privileged to see. I'll keep him all for myself. This one is the Prince your country needs. Strong. Eternal. The greatest prince Lasserno will ever have.'

That praise filled him. Her love, and how freely she gave it, was boundless. He swooped her up, swung her into his arms. She shrieked, and then started giggling.

'What are you doing?'

'Taking this somewhere more comfortable.'

He moved to the seating area he'd installed in this place. Nothing wanting, for her at least.

Every comfort available to her. If this was to be her studio, it had to be perfect. Given the time she spent down here, he hoped it was.

He placed her gently on the large, soft sofa in the corner. Knelt in front of her. Kissed her pregnant belly. Her hand moved to his head, stroked through his hair. He shut his eyes and savoured her touch. One quiet moment of perfection in an otherwise long day. There had been so many small moments like this and Alessio relished each one.

When he opened his eyes Hannah's head tilted to the side, as if she were trying to peer inside him. He could hold no secrets. She owned them all.

'Have you spoken to Stefano?'

Ah. The one wound that remained unhealed. The only ache that hadn't gone away. Being more open with the media now, Alessio saw what Stefano had tried to do. Lasserno *was* happier when shown their leader openly caring. In that way, he'd been right.

'I've tried.'

'You're writing him missives, aren't you?'

Hannah knew him too well. In some things, change came slowly. 'He may not want to speak to the man, but he *will* answer to his Prince. His family always has. It's treasonous to do otherwise.'

'Allow him his pride. He'll answer when the time's right. Anyway, I don't answer you a lot of the time. Am I committing treason too?' Her lips curled into a sultry smile.

'That's to my benefit. You remind me I'm only human, and that's all I have to be.'

Hannah's hand drifted to her belly and all he could see was their future, bright and brilliant.

'I love the human side,' she said.

Alessio trailed his fingers up her legs and she shivered under his touch, goosebumps peppering her skin. 'I love it when you're wearing a skirt.'

'I know.' Her legs parted and his hands drifted higher, his thumbs circling on her inner thighs, her body pliant as it sank into the softness of the sofa.

'I love it even better when you're wearing nothing at all,' he said.

'Rule number two, I seem to remember.'

'What about rule number one?'

She rolled her eyes. 'I didn't promise to obey you when we married. But I did promise to love you.'

Alessio laughed. There was so much laughter in his life now. Hannah brought it into every day. Yes, there was plenty of work too, but there was still play. She could infuse even the difficult times with a sense of fun.

'I love *you*,' he said. Those three words never seemed enough for the bone-deep sentiment they carried. He was aware of the privilege and the trust she'd shown him by saying *yes*. Alessio ensured she knew it every day, so there could be no doubt she'd made the right choice in choosing him.

She cupped his face and the look she gave him could have cut him off at the knees, so it was good that he was kneeling right now. Her eyes were soft, brimming with emotion. So much emotion. He could constantly worship her…it was no trial at all.

'I love you even more.'

He took her hand, running his thumb over her wedding ring and her engagement ring. The ring, which he'd had made especially for her. Their love was so bright and new he wanted gems to reflect that truth. Reflect her. A large emerald the colour of her eyes, flanked by two rubies, the colour of his endless love.

'Never doubt my feelings.'

'I never do.'

He smiled again, slipped his hands into the warm silk of her hair. Alessio relished the lifetime of these moments ahead of them. A future which held her in it was one to anticipate and cherish. Then he dropped his mouth to hers. Kissed her welcoming lips. And spent the afternoon in this pavilion, once built to love, proving their words to be true.

* * * * *